CUTTER

UNCUT

J. WOODBURN

BARNEY

An AppalachianAcorn Book

© Copyright 2022 by J. Woodburn Barney

ISBN 9798402824201

PUBLISHED BY APPALACHIANACORN

COVER PHOTOGRAPH BY JORDAN CALLAHAM
COVER ILLUSTRATION AND DESIGN BY
TAD BARNEY

FOR THE FRIENDS WHO ALWAYS PICKED ME FIRST
FOR THEIR TEAM AND WHO ALWAYS HAD MY BACK.

FOR WELLER AND BECKETT CALLAHAM,
MAY YOU ALWAYS HAVE THOSE KINDS OF FRIENDS.

FOR JOHN SMITH BARNEY, MY TWIN, AND THE FIRST BEST
FRIEND I EVER HAD.

AND FOR MY BEST FRIEND, DEBORAH VARNER.

Also by J. Woodburn Barney

Cutter
Cutter Director's Cut
Cutter Devil's Cut

Time it was, and what a time it was,

It was a time of innocence,

A time of confidences

Long ago, it must be,

I have a photograph

Preserve your memories;

they're all that's left you.

Paul Simon

PROLOGUE

The boy came out of the beater pickup truck, sliding across a seat held together with duct tape, and bounced onto the ground. The old F-150 had been the utility truck at his uncle's place until it became too unreliable for farm use, at which point his uncle sold it to the boy. It was the boy's only real possession, even though some of the guys made fun of it. His family couldn't afford to buy him a car, especially one like most of his friends had. He was a couple inches under six feet, lanky with a mop of dark brown hair which fell almost to his eyes. If someone ran across his senior picture in the yearbook, they would invariably pass over it, one more face in a book of faces. He felt awkward and unattractive. He knew he wasn't cool and cool was what it took to get the girl. He didn't even have a girlfriend. The girl he liked, Regan, was always nice to him, but then she was always nice to everybody. He had thought maybe she would go out with him, but he was afraid to ask. Instead, she dated the lawyer's son. To him, she was just another girl. It wasn't right. He had driven over forty miles on back roads to get here. He didn't want anyone to know where he had come from or why he was here. He took out his wallet before he walked into the fairgrounds building and double checked his money. Seven-hundred eighty dollars. Every penny he had. It had taken him five months of before and after school jobs to save it up. He didn't know if it would be enough to get exactly what he wanted, but he had researched it and thought it would do. He pushed through the door of the old building and was greeted by an armed guard who asked for his driver's license. The boy pulled the license out of his wallet, trying not to let the guard see the wad of money stuffed in there.

1

The guard looked over the license sternly, then smiled, handed it back to the boy and said, "Welcome to the Cedar County Gun Show." The boy nodded and walked into the rows and rows of tables keeping his head down. He surveyed the entire room, trying to find anyone who might recognize him. He saw no one, but then he had not expected to. This show traveled from county to county and would be in his home county in a couple of weeks. Any of those farmers looking for a rifle to rid his place of coyotes or groundhogs would wait until then to go gun shopping. Same story for someone wanting a handgun or sporting weapon. If there was anybody in his town who was a serious collector, they'd skip this show entirely. This was pure backwoods stuff.

He wandered down one row of tables, always asking permission before he picked up a gun to inspect. He made a show of appearing interested in several hunting rifles and an old style Colt six shooter, just like the toy gun he had played cowboys with as a kid. He wondered if that toy was still packed away with the other remnants of his youth. In the second row, he found what he was looking for. An AR-15 assault rifle. The guy selling them had four on display, along with numerous magazines of various capacities. "Can I see that one, sir?" the boy asked, pointing to the oldest looking one. The dealer looked up at the kid and frowned.

"That's a pretty serious weapon, Son. You think you can handle it?" The dealer was dressed in jungle fatigues, like many of his cohorts, and wore a bandanna on his head and a permanent scowl on his face. "You ever shot a gun?"

"Yessir. My father's shotgun and his hunting rifle. We go deer hunting together," he lied.

2

"Well, Son, this is an entirely different kind of rifle. It's not for amateurs."

"Can I shoot it? You know, try it out?"

"There's a range out back, but you'll have to wait until I can go back there with you. And you'll have to buy the ammo." The dealer paused. "How old are you?"

"Twenty-one," the boy lied again.

"Good enough. Come back in about twenty minutes and we'll go blow a hole in a target or two."

The boy noted the time and continued down the row of tables. Every time he saw a similar weapon, he would take out a scrap of paper, write down the table number and the price. He found about a dozen assault rifles for sale by the time the twenty minutes were up. He made his way back to the first dealer. By then, a woman had joined the dealer behind the table and when the boy appeared, the dealer lifted the rifle, two clips of ammo and put them down in front of the boy. "Sixteen dollars." The boy dug out a twenty, got his change and picked up the rifle. "Follow me." The dealer led the kid out the back and down to the makeshift range. He set him up in a firing station and demonstrated how the weapon worked. The boy's hands shook as he hefted the gun to his shoulder. He took a couple of deep breaths and calmed himself. Even with the noise suppressing headphones, the clamor was almost deafening. The boy could not believe how powerful the weapon felt and how powerful it made him feel. In front of him the target jumped and tore to shreds as if it were being blown up from within, as if his actions did not contribute to its destruction.

3

Forty minutes later the boy walked out with the rifle, four 30-round clips and 400 rounds of ammunition. He still had over one hundred dollars left. He sat and thought for several minutes, then put his purchases under the front seat of the truck and went back into the show. He made his way back to the table with the old style six shooter and haggled the seller down to the one hundred dollars in his wallet. He got the guy to throw in a small box of bullets for it. He returned to his truck and though he wasn't sure why, he started to cry, quietly and then in sobs. His shoulders shook and he gripped the steering wheel tightly to regain control. After he calmed himself, he drove slowly back to the Quad Cities.

That night, he lay in bed staring at the ceiling. His friend was sound asleep in the other bed, making those god-awful sleep noises he always made. His friend, the one everyone liked better. He was as much to blame as anyone else. The boy had spent his entire life trying to live up to impossible standards. His family. His stepdad. The guys he hung out with, the ones who always made fun of him. It wasn't fair.

Tomorrow they would all be made to understand. What he was going to do wasn't right. He knew that in his head. And even more so in his heart. He just could not go on like this. They would never understand. They would never accept him. He could look out over his life to come and see no difference from what he had already seen. He would always be second rate. No one would ever give him a chance. Wasn't it bad enough he was poor and homely? And now this insurmountable problem.

But he would even things up. He'd learned how to deal with this. He'd learned the hard way. Olsen had taught him and he had learned the lesson.

4

The next morning, he rose before the sun, even though in May the sun was up early. He dressed and drove to the local doctor's office where he worked in the mornings cleaning up the blood and spittle and mucus and shit from last night's patients. He mopped the floors and took the refuse down to be burned in the incinerator. It smelled bad in the trash bags, worse when it was burned. But it was just this one last time. As he left, he thought to himself, why did I even bother?

He drove to school. He had spent too much time cleaning the lab at the doctor's office and was late, but didn't really care. He had planned to wait in the parking lot until first period had begun anyway. He heard the class bell for first period and the commotion of folks moving from homeroom to their first class. His class would be in the chemistry lab. It's where he would start. And probably end.

He got out of the truck and stripped off his work shirt, down to the black tee he had just bought for the occasion. He got the rifle out of the tool box, slapped a clip into the gun and loaded his pockets with the three remaining clips. One-hundred twenty rounds. He tucked the six shooter into his waistband. More than enough. He wiped his eyes. He could not figure out why tears were blurring his vision. He sat back down in the truck.

PART ONE

CHAPTER ONE

I grumbled down the stairs and punched the "on" button of the coffeemaker. I got the biggest cup I could find in the cupboard and measured out a quarter teaspoon of *magic mushroom elixir* into the bottom of the cup. I didn't really believe in all that magic mushroom crap, but Rachel did and it was just easier to go along than to fight. Actually I had zero information that such things didn't work, but as you know, I am a cynic in both word and deed. The coffee dripped into the carafe and as soon as it looked enough to fill the cup, I poured it. The rest of the pot would be weak, but so what. I was tired of waiting.

I turned on the *Today Show* just in time to hear Savannah read the news headlines. I had to look twice at her outfit. She's a contemporary and smart, attractive and charming, but I swear to God, she has the worst fashion sense in the history of TV. A TV history which includes the fashion statements of Pee-wee Herman and Jed Clampett. This morning's dress set a new standard—it was some color halfway between orange and yellow with huge green flowers and puffy shoulders obviously too big even for Savannah's frame. I chortled coffee into my nose and spit it out onto the counter.

As I was wiping up my mess, Rachel walked into the kitchen, slapped me on the butt and hoarsely whispered, "Mornin', Paleface." She always brought a smile to my face. She made herself a cup of tea, something that smelled like licorice, and carefully measured out and stirred in her magic mushroom elixir. She slid onto the stool next to mine. "So what's your girlfriend Savannah telling us this morning?"

"More useless news about the COVID." Rachel said calling it "the COVID" made me sound like a hillbilly so of course I only referred to this plague we were suffering through as "the COVID". "Apparently the CDC has announced a for-sure completion date for the vaccine, but you know how that is." It had only been a couple of years since we had the vaccine for KM1 and you remember how that all went down. I found it harder and harder to believe anything my government said. If you haven't an idea what I'm talking about, stop reading, go back and read the book J. Woodburn Barney and I wrote about it. Or not.

"Cutter, why do you have to be so negative? I don't think you know how difficult it is sometimes to be around your pessimism." She actually sounded a little hurt, so I backed off. We talked about our plans for the day which mostly consisted of trying to find new ways of avoiding boredom and staying active. And, of course, watching whatever binge series we were currently wrapped up in. But as I went through the day, mowing the yard, masking up for a trip to the hardware store, rewiring an old lamp and masking up again for a trip back to the hardware store to get yet another part (I had about forty dollars in this project to repair a twenty dollar lamp), I mulled over why I was such a cynic. It didn't run in my family, except for maybe Grandpa Williams, but then he was an Iowa farmer and it was a requirement of the job.

It had to go back to my youth. I had a large and loving family. Sure, lots and lots of sibling rivalry (We didn't call it that. We called it fighting with your brothers and sisters), but we had enough food and clean clothes and parents who loved us. And you're a kid. You don't know what you don't have. There was no internet, no cell phones. There was cable TV but not out in the country around DeWitt, Iowa. If you were lucky, and I was, you had a bike and enough empty pop bottles to turn into a little spending cash—that, along with your weekly allowance of a dollar, would go a long way.

There were eight of us. Plus the parents. I was the third from the youngest. John was ten years older than I; then Patti nine years older; Jim, seven years older; Tad, six years; Chris, two years; then me; one year later Tim; and bringing up the rear one year after Tim, was Cathy Rose. Eight kids. Twelve years. My mom, bless her soul, was pregnant all the time. By the time Tim was born, the only way she could walk was to waddle. We were, you'll be shocked to hear, Catholics. My parents practiced the rhythm and blues form of birth control. I'm not complaining. If they'd believed in birth control they probably would have stopped at Jim, maybe Tad. And where would that have left me?

We lived on a dairy farm. Right in the middle of corn and hog country, so we were kind of the odd man out. Grandpa and Dad always had to sit in the back at the Grange meetings and when baling season came, there was no one else to help out. Pigs don't eat a lot of hay. The farm belonged to my mom's family, the Wellers. Hence my middle name. Winston Weller Williams. Helluva moniker to give a kid who lives in the middle of the heartland. But I suppose by the time they got to me, my parents had run out of good names. I had convinced my teachers to call me Win. My family, for reasons unknown, called me Cutter.

Grandpa Weller had inherited the farm, which had been in the family for five generations, when he was just nineteen years old. He was one of three sons, but both of his brothers were killed in World War I. They died days apart in the summer of 1918 when Grandpa was just five years old. My great grandmother Weller never really recovered, and she and my great grandfather died in a car accident in 1932 when she drove their Ford into a farm pond. There were rumors for years she had done it on purpose. I tell you this because Grandpa Weller remained the most upbeat person I ever knew. Even after he lost his own wife which left him on his own with three kids still in their teens.

That was my mom, Ida, and her two brothers. The kids helped run the farm until the brothers both hit eighteen and took off to find their fortunes somewhere other than in a cow's udder. So Grandpa Weller took on a hired hand, a kid from a farm in the next county over, name of Henry Williams. My dad. Henry was ten years older than my mom and was a confirmed bachelor at the ripe old age of 26. It didn't take mom long to notice the kid with the red hair and broad shoulders stacking hay in her barn. She spent the next five years changing his mind about the benefits of bachelorhood and they were married in 1959. They helped Grandpa Weller run the farm and after several years of trying, and after the family doctor prescribed boxers to replace the tighty whities, began a decade of cranking out babies in 1964. As the family grew, Grandpa Weller and Dad would add another room to the already sprawling farmhouse. When I was born, Grandpa declared if there was one more kid born, he was moving the kids into the barn and the cows into the house.

You got all that? 'Cause in about fifty pages there will be a test on my genealogy. Maybe. What Holden called "all that David

Copperfield kind of crap." The dates and the names really aren't important. We were country farm folk and we thought life was pretty grand. We learned everything about the world we needed to know from our town or from our TV—old people farmed or sat on a bench downtown or they lived in Florida like the Golden Girls; all doctors were African American, based on Dr. Huxtable and our own Dr. Branham; city teenagers were like the kids on *Family Ties, Growing Pains* or *Facts of Life;* and rich people drank a lot. When we weren't doing chores or in school, we played sports in their proper season, we played board games in crappy weather and we marked down the days until our birthdays, Halloween and Christmas.

I believe what we are is determined by those broad strokes of genetics and environment, so I broke really lucky from the get go. But how we see the world. That can be determined by the smallest, seemingly insignificant moments. All that Robert Frost "Two roads diverged in a yellow wood" horse hockey. At the time it was just something that happened in school starting in the fourth grade. Only later did it take on significance. Only after Charlie and I became best friends.

CHAPTER TWO

"Class," Sister Mary Elizabeth hushed us with the single word. Fourth grade and up to this point we had had only lay teachers at St. Joseph's Elementary School. But it hadn't taken long for us, all 32 of us in fourth grade, to learn why nuns were so feared. Sister Mary even whispering a classmate's name had caused reactions from crying to wetting your pants. It was hard to believe that in the supposedly enlightened 80s, teachers were still allowed to pinch an ear, pull hair, or rap knuckles with a wooden ruler... but in fact they did.

"Class, I would like you to welcome our newest student, Charles Settler. Charles' family just moved to Dewitt and he and his family have joined our congregation. Please say 'Hello' to him."

In unison we all said, mostly lacking enthusiasm, "Hello, Charles."

"Charles, please say 'Hello' to your new classmates."

Nothing. Charles Settler shuffled his feet, stared at the floor and turned bright red. He was a little kid. Straight brown hair shaped into a mutilated bowl cut, like someone had literally put a bowl on his head and cut everything that hung out and then someone had tried to fix it with kids' scissors and failed miserably. He said nothing.

"Charles! Say 'Hello'." Sister's request had become an order. We all slunk down in our seats.

"H-h-h-h-h-h-h-h-lo." We all looked at the tops of our desks or out the window or at our hands. It was eerily quiet. I peeked up and it looked like Charles was going to cry. I looked away quickly.

"Charles, please take a seat back there next to Winston in the third row. Since it was the only empty seat in the room, Charles had no problem finding it. He sat down, put his head on the desk and I heard him sniffle. I looked straight ahead, silently glad it wasn't me who had gone through that. Some of my classmates stifled laughs or giggles and it made me hate them for a minute. Though I wasn't sure why.

At recess, the squad gathered, as it always did on these warm early May days, to play softball. We called ourselves *the squad* though I can't remember how or why that started. There were nine of us, enough for one team, though mostly we couldn't find anyone else to play against, except for a couple of the dweebs, so we took whatever outliers we found and divided into teams. The squad was Fat Jimmy Hendricks; Dave the Brain Snyder; Sweet Willie Rawers; the Dunlap twins, Randy and Andy; Red Palmer (whose real name was Lynne and yeah, she was a girl, but she had an arm like a cannon and could hit from both sides of the plate); Neal Booger Conners; me and my brother Tim who we called Tiny Tim. It had taken us four years to come up with all those names and to this day that's how I still think of them.

As we headed out to the playground, Randy yelled at me, "Hey, Cu-Cu-Cu-Cu-Cu-Cu-Cutter. What's it like havin' to sit next to the dink? He get any hockers on you?" Most of the squad started laughing until Red punched Randy in the chest and told him to shut up. She gave everyone the evil eye. We hung our heads. Nobody wanted to get on Red's bad side. She was not above running you over on the base path or chucking one at your head. We found three of the dweebs already at our makeshift ballfield, chose up sides and got in a good three innings before the bell rang. On the way back in, I saw Charles sitting on the steps where he had spent the entire

14

recess by himself. The rest of the afternoon the class, including me, just ignored the new kid. He never spoke again.

After the school day ended, we hustled outside to jostle for position in the bus line, on accounta there would be few good seats left and you didn't want to get stuck sitting next to some dweeb from Ekstrand Elementary. St. Joe's didn't have any buses of their own, so we all rode the city's school buses. Those kids got picked up first so we always got last choice of seats. We were collectively called "Snaps" by the townies, a shortened version of the derogatory name for Catholics, Mackerel Snappers. In the greater scheme of things, no kid from DeWitt was a society hot shot, but even in DeWitt there were distinct class lines. And being a Catholic kid who lived in the country put me in one of the lower classes. Had I not been a pretty fair baseball player, I would have been even lower.

I noticed Charles was looking a little lost until a nun pointed out the line I was in. He walked over, never looking up and got in line behind me. He didn't even complain when Tim came up and jumped in front of me. It was a brother thing—we held places for each other in line. And brother Chris who was in sixth grade showed up, Cathy Rose in hand, and pushed in front of Tim. About the same time two younger, round-faced and scraggly looking kids came running up. They both looked like Charlie Brown from Peanuts, even the little girl. When she saw Charles, she squealed and ran up and hugged him tightly. He returned the hug and thumped the little boy on the shoulder. It was the first time he smiled all day.

We boarded the bus and shoved our way into seats. Booger, the only other kid in the squad who rode our bus had saved me a seat, though he was one of the first off since he lived at the edge of town. Charles and his kids shuffled past me and I snuck a peek back to see where he sat. The three couldn't find a seat together, but I saw Charles and the little girl sitting across the aisle from each other and they were holding hands. I looked away before he could catch me spying on him. By the time the bus was a mile out of town, lots of kids had gotten off and we all spread out to get more comfortable. We lived a little less than five miles from town and I noticed when we got off, Charles and the kids were still in the back of the bus.

The next morning when we got on the bus, there was Charles with the two little kids, sitting together in the backseat. We didn't acknowledge each other, though I saw him point at me and say something to the little girl. She smiled. She was wearing the same dress she had on the day before, but her hair was combed and there was a ribbon in it. She looked happy, little-kid-each-day-is-an-adventure happy.

Throughout the following week, nothing changed. We rode the bus together, we sat next to each other in class, he sat by himself at recess and lunch and the only times he was forced to talk by the nuns, he stuttered. When any other kid made an effort to engage him, he generally answered with a head nod or shake, sometimes a "y-y-y-y-ea" or mostly likely a "n-n-n-n-n-n-n-n-o." They soon gave up. It had probably been five days and the seat Booger saved for me on the ride home was right in front of Charles and the little kids. That's when I eavesdropped and learned the kids were his younger brother and sister, neither of them stuttered and, most shockingly, when he talked to them, he didn't stutter either.

When we were about a mile from my house, I got up the nerve to say to him, mind you, not look at him, but to say, "Why don't you have any problems talking with the kids?" Pretty rude, right? Understand I was a ten year old kid and my filters weren't formed yet. (When Rachel read this she pointed out that apparently they never did.) Charles said nothing but before I could tell him "sorry", his sister said, "Oh, Charlie just gets nervous around new people and it makes him stutter. I'm Carol. What's your name?"

By this time I had turned to look at them and I told her, "Cutter."

She looked at me like I was some weird species of bug and said, "That's a stupid name."

Even before I could laugh, Charles snapped at her, "Carol, that's not nice. Tell him you're sorry." I was shocked. Stunned. Not one skipped or repeated sound.

By now I was completely turned around in my seat facing them. I told her, "Oh, Carol. That's okay. It is a stupid name." She and I and the other brother (whose name turned out to be Jimmie) all laughed. Charles just turned red. The bus lurched to a stop and my brother Chris yelled at me that it was our house. I grabbed my backpack, waved at Carol and hurried down the aisle.

CHAPTER THREE

A couple of days later, I was again in the seat in front of Charles and his brother and sister. After most of the kids had gotten off, Charles tapped me on the shoulder and asked, "Cu-Cu-Cu-Cu-tter, d-d-d-do you guys ever let s-s-s-someone new play ball with you?"

"Sure, Charles..." He interrupted me.

"Eh-eh-eh-it's Charlie."

"Sure, Charlie, anybody can play. Ya just gotta show up at the field at recess. It's not like real baseball on accounta we're not allowed to use hardballs at school, but it's okay." He nodded and smiled.

The next morning on the bus, Charlie was not sitting with his brother and sister. He was in the seat across from them. When Chris, Tiny Tim and I got on, Charlie waved me back to where he was sitting. As I sat, he held up an old Sears and Roebuck Ted Williams glove. "I-I-I-I-I." He stopped, shook his head and sorta slapped his cheek. He tried again, "I-I-I brought my glove. It's real old. Usta be my-my-my brother Woody's. Is it okay for you guys?"

"Heck, yeah." I took the glove, slipped it on and pounded the pocket a couple of times. "Nice," I added. Charlie smiled.

At recess, he walked with me to the makeshift ballfield but kinda hung back when we got there. I yelled out to the squad, "Hey, Charlie's gonna play with us, okay?"

True to form, Randy yelled back, "O-o-o-o-o-o-o-k." Also true to form, Red punched him in his throwing shoulder. He flinched and whined, "Hey, that hurt."

Red said "Told ya," and drew back her fist again. Randy backed down to the hoots and hollers of the rest of the squad.

I think I may have mentioned I was a pretty fair ball player. I was no Red Palmer, but I was a close enough second that she and I always got to be captains. She threw a bat up in the air, I caught it by the barrel and held it out, handle up. She put her hand above mine and we climbed hand over hand up the barrel and handle until someone could get their thumb on the knob—that person got to choose first. Today, that was me. I picked Sweet Willy first 'cause he was the best infielder in the group, then Booger 'cause he always saved me a seat. On my third pick, I took Charlie 'cause I didn't want him to feel bad. Sweet Willy rolled his eyes at me, but Red smiled. I wasn't sure if it was because she thought it was the right thing to do or because she was sure I'd made a bad pick.

I'm no dummy. Until a kid shows he can play, you stick them with the other dweebs out in the outfield. I put Charlie in right field. It's softball. No one hits to right field except for bad players or left handers, and the only left hander was Dave the Brain and he was on our side. By the third inning, no balls had gone to Charlie. Then Red got up, and instead of batting righty, she switched to the other side of the plate and hit my first pitch deep into right field. Crap.

Charlie was moving before the ball left the infield. He got to the ball almost on the foul line and snagged it on the run, an over-the-shoulder, one-handed catch. Booger, playing third, started cheering. Randy, who had been on second, tagged up and headed towards Booger. Charlie whirled around and threw the hardest thrown ball I had ever seen towards third. A bullet. When Randy got there, Booger was standing on the base with a smile on his face and the ball in his hand. Double play. Just as the recess bell rang. As near as I can remember, Randy never made fun of Charlie again.

Charlie didn't really become a part of the squad, but he was there any time a ballgame was going on. He was always the first person picked, and it had nothing to do with anyone feeling sorry for him. He was not only good in the field but could also smack the ball around the diamond on command. Once we picked teams, the game would go on for six innings, no matter how many recesses it took. The next three times we picked teams, Red always got first pick. I accused her of cheating, until she threatened to punch me as well. So it was about three weeks before Charlie and I were on the same team again.

Charlie loosened up with the kids, but he never got a whole sentence out in class without stuttering badly. Sister Mary Elizabeth, who we called Witch Sister, never let up on him in class. She would call on him and as soon as he started stuttering, she would make him stop answering, even if he knew the answer. And would then give him failing grades for class participation. She told him it was all in his head. Which it was, I guess. We got our final grades the weekend before classes ended for the year. Charlie shared his card on the way home. Cs in everything—As on tests, Fs on participation. It didn't seem fair.

Charlie didn't show up for the last Monday of class. On the bus, I asked Carol where he was. She said he was sick and would say no more. Jimmie wouldn't answer when I asked what was wrong with Charlie. The next day, none of them were on the bus. I figured he must have something bad 'cause we had explained to him how those last few days the recesses were extra-long and we got to play a lot of softball. And then it was baseball season for little league and this was our first year of kid pitch. Tryouts were on the last day of school, at the school. Charlie was gonna be our secret weapon in our ongoing battle with the townies.

After school the day before the tryouts, I told Tiny Tim we had to go find Charlie and make sure he came to school the next day. We lived out on 270th Street, which was really a series of unconnected dead end roads. The county never wanted to pay for the bridges to connect a few farms and some swamp land, so you couldn't go from one end to the other without backtracking onto 262nd Street. Which is what our bus did after it dropped us off.

Charlie had told me that they lived "in the old Horner place out off Two Six Two". I asked my dad if he knew where that was.

"You mean Old Man Horner's old farm?"

"I dunno."

"I can't believe anyone could live in that house. I think it's been empty for several years. And it was falling down when Old Man Horner lived there. That old man was so tight he'd rather sit in the rain in his bedroom than spend five bucks on a roof patch." My dad just shook his head.

"Well? Where is it?"

"Go out to 262, turn right and go about a mile to a gravel lane on the right. The house is back that lane 'bout half a mile." Charlie had told me they had a long walk once they got off the bus. It meant it was about a 20 minute ride each way, maybe more if his lane was gravelly. Tim and I got our bikes out of the barn, waved at Dad as he warned, yet again, to be careful and I yelled we'd be back in an hour.

"What do you think is wrong with Charlie?" Tim asked as we rode out 270th.

"I dunno. Probably the flu or something. Maybe they all have it so we should not get too close. Unless he's feeling better." Our conversation turned to baseball tryouts. It was gonna be Tim's last year of coach pitch so we wouldn't be on the same team. He was pretty excited to be one of the big kids on his team. And not have to share the field with me. I got that. I'd gone through the same thing with Chris for a couple of years.

We got to Charlie's lane and turned in. It was pretty overgrown and dusty, like it hadn't been used much. About a quarter mile down, it ran through a dry creek bed, which probably would be a mess to go through when it rained hard, and there were dense woods on the right. It was kinda spooky, to tell you the truth. I peddled faster and Tim yelled I was kicking up dust in his face.

We got down to the house which indeed did look deserted, except for the old truck and some toys in the front yard. The two-story farmhouse had a big wraparound porch and you could see missing boards from the railing. It hadn't been painted in years and was all a dull gray. I half decided my plan was stupid and turned to tell Tim we should probably just go home when Carol came busting out of the house, smiling and yelling, "Cutter. Tim. Whada you guys doin' here?" She practically bounced off the porch and down to our bikes.

"Hey, Carol. We came to see Charlie." The smile left her face. She looked back towards the house just as the screen door opened and a

woman stepped out. "Mom. Cutter and Tim are here to see Charlie."
Mrs. Settler smiled and walked down the steps to greet us.

"Boys, Charlie and Jimmie and Carol have told me all about you.
It's nice to finally meet you. I take it you live close?"

"Uh," was about all I could get out. Mrs. Settler was tall and thin
with lots of dark hair. And really pretty. You know, for a mom and
all.

Tim broke in. "We're here to see Charlie. Tomorrow is tryouts for
little league and he's the best player we've got. He's even better than
Red and she's great. Charlie's got to be there." I nodded my head in
agreement.

Mrs. Settler frowned and then smiled again. "Oh boys, I'm sorry.
Charlie is under the weather and he just can't go to school tomorrow.
I'm sure he'll feel better in a few days. I'll have him call you then. Is
there any way he can try out later?"

I was ten. Everything that was important to me was urgent. Like it
is to every ten year old. It had never occurred to me if a guy was sick
that maybe he could try out later. So I told her, "I dunno. I can ask."

"That would be very nice of you, Tim."

"Oh, that's Tim," I said, pointing at my brother. "I'm Cutter." She
looked confused, so I tried to explain, "My real name is Win, short
for Winston, but everyone except the nuns call me 'Cutter'." She
smiled again and it made me smile. She was the prettiest mom I had
ever seen. "We'll ask."

"Thank you, Cutter." She dipped her head towards me. "I know
Charlie would thank you as well. Let me get a piece of paper so I can
write down your phone number." She turned and walked into the

house. She was back out to us in a minute, I told her our phone number, she thanked us again and she walked back into the house.

Carol, who had not said a word since her mom came out, asked us, " Do you think you guys could come play some time? And bring Cathy Rose?" We both nodded yes and climbed back on our bikes. Carol waved and we started up the lane. I looked over my shoulder at the house and saw Charlie in an upstairs window. It was kinda dark where he was but I saw him wave. I stopped and waved back.

Chapter Four

When my son Livingston decided he wanted to play tee ball, Rachel (also lovingly referred to as She-Who-Must-Be-Obeyed...though never out loud) decreed I should volunteer to coach. It was then that I learned something which rocked the very foundation of my childhood. "Tryouts" for little league weren't really tryouts. I mean, we went and threw and caught the ball, we ran around the bases, we fielded grounders and fly balls and we batted. But no one was ever not taken for a team. Everyone, including the dweebs and the booger eaters and the dorks, everyone made it onto a team. No one was cut. But when you are ten years old, you are so nervous before tryouts, you can't eat, you can't sleep, you can't think about anything else. What if I flub up, drop a fly ball, fall down running the bases, strike out at the plate? What if I'm not good enough? I had played before and knew I was good, but anything might go wrong at a tryout.

So, when I got to tryouts the next day, I had completely forgotten about asking if Charlie could try out after he got better. I did great. Caught everything that came my way, ran fast, hit the first three pitches into the outfield. I was elated. And relieved. My brothers Tim and Chris also did well and when Dad picked us up, we were excited and hungry. He took us for ice cream. I got the chocolate vanilla swirl. The big one. As we sat at the picnic table, Dad asked, "Did your coach say it was okay for your friend Charlie to try out later?"

I just stared at him. The ice cream started to melt and run down my hand. How could I have forgotten? I didn't just let Charlie down.

I had let the whole team down. I didn't know what to do. I didn't, but I felt like crying. "Dad, what should I do? I totally forgot."

Dad kinda laughed and told me, "I think we can fix it." We drove back to the park, found the still kibitzing coaches. (I thought they were just shooting the ole crappola. In fact they were dividing the teams up so each team got some good players and some dorks and dweebs.) I jumped out of the car and ran over to the coach who was gonna run the Catholic school team.

"Coach Weaver."

"Yes, Win?"

"Coach, I forgot to ask you. My friend Charlie Settler has been sick and couldn't come to tryouts. Is there any way he can still make our team? He's in my class at school and he's good enough to play for us." Coach Weaver just stared at me. "Please."

"Sure, Win. I think we can make a place for him on the team. Have him come to our first practice. We'll give him a chance." He smiled and punched me in the arm and pulled down the bill of my ball cap. I vowed to myself to never screw up like that again. If you've read my other stories, you know I have broken that oath about a gazillion times.

There is no day like the first day of summer vacation. The whole glorious summer stretches out in front of you. Baseball games. Trips to the creek to swim and fish. Wiener roasts. Bike trips to town for ice cream. Spending some time away from the family to visit the Williams grandparents' farm where you got to be king for a few days. Making forts in the woods behind our place. And, sure, there were daily chores but that first day. That first day you didn't have to do anything. You slept in. You ate cereal in front of the TV. You went to the barn and found a place in the hay mow to lay back and celebrate your good fortune. You never had one thought about school.

Two days later Mrs. Settler called my mom and asked if Tim and I could come over to play with her kids. After Mom's stern warnings to be on our best behavior, we grabbed our mitts, climbed on our bikes and pedaled the 20 minutes to their house. When we got there, Charlie, Jimmie and Carol were all sitting on the steps to the front door. Carol was up and running to us before we could park our bikes (and by park, I mean fling to the ground). She gave each of us a quick hug and laughed. For a little kid, and a girl, she wasn't too bad.

The guys stayed seated and we gave each other the universal guy greeting.

"Hey."

"Hey."

Jimmie and Tiny Tim joined in with their renditions. "Hey," and "Hey."

We walked over and sat down on the steps, me next to Charlie and Tim next to Jimmie. Charlie was sitting all the way over to the edge of the steps and when he talked he stared straight ahead and wouldn't look at me. "Hey, Cu-cu-cu-cu-cu-cutter. Th-th-thanks for getting me on the team. Th-th-the coach called my mom and told her."

"No problem. I almost forgot but then I remembered," I sorta lied.

"So what are we gonna do?" Carol asked.

Her mom answered from inside the house. "We're gonna bake cookies. The boys don't want their little sister messing up their fun."

"Aw, Mom, I never get to do anything fun. Cutter's my friend too, aren't you?" She looked at me hopefully.

"You betcha, Carol, but it would be great if you could bake some cookies with your mom. She sounds like she really needs the help." Carol looked dejected. She hung her head and walked to the front door. I called after her, "But maybe later we could play Monopoly or something."

"That'd be great. And I don't think Cutter is a stupid name." She went inside.

"So whadya wanta do?" Tim asked.

Jimmie pointed further down their lane to some woods. "We could go mess around down at the creek." Since no one else had any other suggestions, we nodded our assent. He yelled into the house, "Mom, we're going over to the woods." No response.

When we stepped out of the shadows of the porch into sunlight, Charlie turned towards me and pointed to the left side of his face. "I-I-I-I kinda banged up my face last week. F-f-f-f-fell on the steps." The whole left side of his face was yellow, a bad bruise which was just healing. There was a small scab under his eye.

"Wow. That sucks. Looks like it hurt a lot."

"Nah. Didn't hurt at all." His head bounced up and down like he was shaking it off.

We walked down past some rundown outbuildings, between a couple of fields where corn was just coming up and into some woods. It was much cooler in the woods and it smelled of semi-stagnant water. Within a couple of minutes we were at a creek and followed it down to where it ran into a small lake. Our farm was about a mile

28

from the Wapsi River—really the Wapsipinicon, but no one called it that and most of the land between our farm and the river was basically swampland with crisscrossing creeks and small lakes. I guessed Charlie's place must be closer to the river.

We horsed around in the water until we were all good and soaked and started looking for crawdads. I asked them, "Do you guys fish here? Is the fishin' any good?"

Jimmie said, "We don't have any fishing poles, so we haven't tried it. Dad says he'll get some for us, but he never has."

"Does your dad farm?" Tim wanted to know.

"Nah," replied Jimmie, "he sometimes does some mechanic's work but says no one will hire him on accounta he doesn't got his own tools. He says it just ain't fair. How's a guy supposed to buy tools if he can't get a job to earn the money to buy them?" We just nodded our heads in agreement.

We headed upstream and came out in a narrow strip of woods where we could see their house over to the right. We walked back into a larger woods and started chucking sticks and kicking plants and looking for bugs or snakes or furry critters. You know, guy woods stuff. About 20 minutes into the woods, Jimmie stopped and pointed at an old fallen down sycamore tree. "Hey, Cutter, look. Isn't that the tree in the woods at the end of our road?"

You have to understand. Nowadays, you reach into your pocket, pull out your cell phone, hit the maps icon and poof, you know where you are and everything around you, from 50 feet away to, well, to the whole world. Back then, maps were something your dad kept in the glove compartment of the car and only looked at when no one else was around. Those maps showed you cities and towns and major roads but you really had no idea, especially as a kid, where things were. You learned the roads and streams and woods by exploring them. You were always a little afraid in the woods that you might get lost, but over time you knew them as well as your own backyard.

"Yeah," I answered. "How 'bout that. We must be lots closer through the woods to Settler's than we are by road. Cool." We walked out to the end of our road to confirm we were where we thought we were. We came up with a plan to make a bike route through the woods and fields from our house to their house.

We took what we thought was the most direct route back to Settler's and ended up there in just a few minutes. This was gonna be a great summer.

CHAPTER FIVE

After we got back to their house, Mrs. Settler fixed us lunch. Peanut butter and jelly on Wonder Bread. It was great. We played catch for an hour or so and then Carol made me play checkers with her on the porch while the other guys went to check out the old barn. The checkers game wasn't too bad. I let her win and got cookies in exchange. Around two o'clock, an old car came barreling down the driveway. I've never seen kids move as fast as Jimmie and Charlie coming out of the barn. They were on the porch panting before the car screeched to a stop, clouds of dust settling on everything.

I looked at Charlie. "It's Dad. H-h-h-he doesn't like us to play in the b-b-b-barn."

A man lots smaller than my father or grandfathers rolled out of the car and waved the dust from the air in front of him. He spat. He came towards the porch and I could have picked him out as Jimmie's dad anywhere. He looked exactly like an older version. Round face, freckles, red hair. Big smile on his face.

"So, who's this?" He nodded towards Tim and me.

Carol answered, "Daddy, this's Cutter and Tim. Remember we told you about them. They go to our school and ride on our bus. Cutter and me are playing checkers and I'm winning." She beamed.

"That's great, Babycakes. Where's your mom?"

"Inside. And we made cookies and they're real good. We saved some for you."

He walked into the house without another word. About a minute later, Mrs. Settler came to the front door and though the screen said to Tim and me, "Boys, it's probably time for you to head home. Thanks for coming over."

Tim asked, "Can Jimmie and Charlie come over to our house tomorrow to play?"

"We'll see." That's mom talk for "no".

The next day we had our mom call Mrs. Settler to ask if Charlie and Jimmie needed a ride to baseball practice. Mrs. Settler told my mom thank you very much because she didn't have a car and didn't know if her husband was going to be home in time to take them.

We picked them up and drove to town for practice. When we got there, the coach gave his coach speech. Which no one listened to 'cause it was always the same. Well, that's not true, Charlie and Jimmie listened 'cause they had never heard it before. Right after the speech about fair play, trying hard, and all that grownup crappola, the coach pulled my brother Chris aside (he's two years older than me and would have been one of the 12 year olds on my team) and asked him if he wanted to move up to Babe Ruth league, which is like the big time. It took Chris zero seconds to say "Yes" which was fine with me. No big brother on the team to cause me misery.

The first practice is when they decide whether you will be a starter, where you are going to play, when you are gonna bat and basically if you're a real player or a dweeb. You do pretty much all the same stuff as tryouts, except more of it. They time you running around the bases. They hit hard grounders and high flies and line drives to see what you can handle. They take you over to the side of the field and have you try pitching. You bat for 15 or 20 pitches.

I really wanted to be a pitcher, but I was one of the youngest on the team so I figured I'd be lucky to start in the outfield.

I was doing okay when they called us new kids to take our turn being timed on running the bases. I was waiting my turn while Charlie took his turn. He seemed to be going really fast, but the coach looked at his stop watch and showed it to the assistant coach who shook his head. They asked Charlie if he would do it again. I heard the coach say apparently he didn't hit the timer on time. Charlie thought he didn't do it fast enough, so he ran harder. This time the coaches watched and smiled when he hit home plate.

Coach Weaver said, "Well, if he can hit at all, we have our leadoff hitter," and patted Charlie on the back. They always put the fastest guy in leadoff on accounta not wanting some slow kid to get run over. Then they sent all the new kids (all of us were from the squad––Randy and Andy, Red, Sweet Willie, me and Charlie) over to try out for pitcher. They had us warm up with each other. Charlie and I took turns pitching and catching. I had caught in coach pitch and liked wearing all the gear and trying to throw kids out who were stealing.

Charlie is throwing really hard, just like he always did, even harder than Red. The assistant coach watches for a while and comes over and takes the mitt away from me and has Charlie pitch to him. He'd move the mitt around and ask Charlie to hit it, which he does every time. The more Charlie throws, the bigger the coach smiles. Finally, he stops and asks Charlie if he has ever pitched before.

Charlie turns red and says "N-n-n-n-n-no. Sir."

I butt in and tell the coach that sometimes when he's nervous Charlie stutters a little. The coach asks me if I've ever caught before and I say "yes" and he says go over to the diamond and try to throw from home to second, which is a snap, of course. Now he's grinning and tells Coach Weaver he has a new starting pitcher and a catcher. And pretty soon he's back with Red saying he has another pitcher and that this is gonna be a big year for the Hawkeyes, which is what our team name is.

After practice, my mom picked us all up. We're tired and dirty and happy, but mostly we're hungry and she agreed to take us to McDonald's. Charlie leaned over and whispered to me that they didn't have any money. I told him no problem it would be my treat, but I didn't have any money either and so when we got there I had to ask Mom if it was okay. It was.

Charlie and Jimmie both ordered happy meals with cheeseburgers. Jimmie told my mom, "I love McDonald's. The hamburgers are so much better than the way Mom makes them." I had to agree but couldn't say anything on accounta my mom being right there. The ones my mom made were thick and dry and too small for the bun.

Mom asked Jimmie, "How does your mother make them?"

Jimmie explained, "Well, she mixes the hamburger up with lots of old bread torn up into little pieces, then she squashes them real flat so when they cook they are really skinny. And they don't taste real good."

Mom said, "Oh they sound fine," but she frowned and I could tell she didn't really think so.

Chapter Six

Over the next couple of practices, Charlie and Red and Jerry and I spent lots of time practicing pitching. Jerry, who was the only black guy on our team, was 12 and had been the number two pitcher last year. This year he would be number one. Red's dad, who always came to every practice and game, called us all up to the stands where he was sitting.

"So, guys," he said. "I've been watching you and you three will be the best pitchers in the league. No doubt. I'm not your coach, but I think you should try to do a couple of things. You should not try any fancy pitches like curve balls. Those will hurt your arms. Your two pitches should be the fast ball and the changeup."

I interrupted, "What's a changeup?"

He smiled. "Well, it looks like the pitch is going to be the same as a fast ball, but it's much slower. Lynne, let's show them."

We all clambered down the bleachers and back on the field. Red showed us how to look like she was gonna throw hard, but the pitch was lots slower. We watched and the only one who said anything was Charlie. "C-c-c-c-cool."

"A couple of more things. And, Cutter, this is important to you, 'cause you don't want your pitchers to be having to do any thinking out there. You want them only to think about the target of your glove. Try always to throw strikes. Don't let them get free passes on you. Throw low balls in the middle of the plate. If they hit it, it will most likely be a grounder which the infielders can get. But if you get two strikes on them, then throw it high. No batter can resist a high pitch and they are impossible to hit."

It turned out to be the best advice we got. After three games we were 3 and 0. Jerry threw a shutout, Charlie had 10 strikeouts in the six inning game and Red won a close game. The only reason it was close, was because she got mad at one of the other team's players who made fun of her being a girl and she "accidentally" hit the kid in the shoulder with a pitch and gave up a couple of runs. My mom and dad came to the games. Charlie's parents couldn't make it. Charlie's oldest brother Woody and his sister Jean and brother Carl, who were a few years older, did come a couple of times. I thought that was pretty neat 'cause none of my older brothers and sisters ever came.

In fact Woody was there midway through the season when Charlie made league history as the youngest player to ever throw a no hitter. Now, if you know anything about little league, it's that no hitters are not all that rare. In fact a kid in our league threw one at the end of the season but ended up losing on accounta his seven walks and his team committing like a gazillion errors. Still, the kid was pretty happy.

Charlie just missed a perfect game and was as close as you can get. Randy and Andy took turns playing first base and we had practiced a pitch out to try to catch a guy leaning the wrong way off first. Anyway, in the fourth inning Charlie gave up a walk and before the next batter came out, Randy called time and went to the mound. I took off my mask and walked out, just like in the big leagues, for a conference. I figured Randy was gonna tell Charlie it was okay and to settle down. Nope, Randy decided it was time to pick a guy off first. And in what became the most memorable moment of my lackluster sports career, two pitches later I picked the guy off first. Charlie only faced 18 batters, the minimum in a six inning game. Not surprising that by the end of the season, the high school baseball coach came to watch Charlie.

But the really important stuff was we laid out a trail between our houses through the woods. It never occurred to us that someone else owned those woods. But no one objected. Actually other than us and our moms, probably no one else knew.

I learned pretty early to avoid manual labor whenever I could. Being one of the youngest kids had few advantages, but one of them was we didn't have many chores. Tim and I were responsible for feeding the chickens, cleaning the hen house once a summer (talk about a really crappy job) and collecting the eggs. The fun part of the egg collection is once in a while you'd find one that was obviously old and when you threw it against the barn, it would make a real loud pop. And stink. Really bad. That was great.

The thing about the trail was that it turned out to be really hard physical labor, but it was so much fun we never noticed. We started at our end and decided to go as straight as we could, meaning not cut down any big trees, towards the Settler house. It didn't take Charlie long to figure out what we should do was find a path which avoided low areas so we wouldn't get our bikes stuck or get all muddy after it rained. About four days later, when we showed up at our end of the woods, he led us along his path which he had marked by putting string on trees. Two days earlier he had gone out in the rain and found the high spots. I would never have figured that out, let alone actually gone out in the rain to do it.

We had to cut out and drag away lots of undergrowth, move some fair-sized fallen logs and bring in some rocks for the dry run we had to cross. It took us half the summer to finish it and the day it was done we celebrated by riding across it to our house and then riding into town for ice cream. Tim proclaimed it would be called "The Iowa Trail" because he had been playing Oregon Trail on our Atari like a madman for the last six months.

Don't get the idea that's all we did. It just made getting back and forth to Settler's a whole lot faster and easier. Charlie and Jimmie would come to our house sometimes, but for the most part, we hung out at their place. For one thing, their dad was rarely at home and our dad always was. And if there is anything my dad hated seeing, it was perfectly able boys not working. Also, our barns were fully used; theirs were mostly ignored and filled with old junk to play with. But mostly, it was because their house was much closer to "The Island".

About 150 yards from Charlie's house towards the Wapsi was mostly swamp land all the way down to the river. It wasn't any good for farming so it was largely ignored. Almost every year, lots of the area was flooded. Not in big floods, the ones our parents and grandparents talked about, always like they were something sacred. "Remember the big one of '47?" or "This is nothing like the flood of '65 or even '69. Now those were real floods." But there were a series of streams and swamps and lakes and it was the best place in the world to be ten years old, especially with buddies. You just wanted to be gone before dusk on accounta the skeeters were as big as houseboats, leastwise according to my mom.

It didn't take us long to find, explore and claim as our own, an island in the middle of one of the larger lakes there. It wasn't exactly a true island 'cause there was a narrow spit of land at the far end which attached it to the woods. But it was close enough to work for us. At first we decided it would be a perfect place for a fort. We tried making one out of sticks and stuff we found there, but then started hauling stuff from the old sheds at Settler's place to make walls and a roof.

We'd gotten walls up and dragged some old pieces of tin for the roof when my week to go to Grandpa and Grandma Williams' farm came up. They lived outside of Anamosa and going from one farm to another wasn't that big of a treat. And they raised hogs, so it always took a day or two to get used to the smell. "Smell? What smell? I don't smell anything," Grandma Williams would always say. But it was part of my grandparents' smell so it never really bothered me.

The best part of the week would be the day Grandma took me into Cedar Rapids for a day of shopping, lunch and a movie. We would shop at Lindale Mall, then go downtown for lunch. She gave me a whole $20 to spend on anything I wanted (it was always toys or sports stuff). I got to pick the restaurant and the movie. It was the one day of the year I was king for a day. Better even than Christmas. Except, of course, when it was Christmas, then that was the best day of the year.

But this year, for the first time ever, I wasn't excited to go. Our adventures in the woods, our construction projects, the fact that we were leading the league in baseball and mostly because we had new friends to hang out with. The day my parents picked me up to go home, they dropped Tim off for his grandparents' week. I couldn't wait to get home and jump on my bike to go see Charlie. When I rode up to the house, I heard lots of yelling and things banging around. It was scary so I just froze in my tracks. Charlie's dad was yelling, "Damnit, woman, if I come home again and dinner is not on the table, I'll give you a lesson you'll never forget. Now get my damn dinner in front of me." And something banged against the wall. Very loud. I jumped on my bike and high-tailed it home.

The next morning I waited until I thought Charlie's dad would have left for work and I rode through the woods to his house. I stopped at the edge of the woods to check for Mr. Settler's car. It was gone so I pedaled on over to the house. Carol was sitting on the porch playing with a doll and I coasted up but didn't get off my bike. "Hey, Carol, is Charlie home?"

"He's inside with mom and the older kids. Mom's having a family meeting but told me to wait out here. She seems real sad."

"Well, tell Charlie I was here, okay?"

Mrs. Settler came to the screen door. "Hey, Carol," she started and then saw me. She smiled and said, "Oh, Cutter. I'm glad you're here. Charlie has been whining for a week that he has nothing to do since you were gone. He'll be glad to see you." And louder, "Charlie, Cutter's here."

Charlie shot out of the house like a cannon. "C'mon, C-c-c-cutter, I gotta show you what I've done to the fort." He jumped off the porch, hit me on the shoulder and picked his bike up off the lawn. "C'mon!"

I followed him down to the edge of the woods where we parked our bikes and hiked towards our island, about ten minutes into the undergrowth. The fort looked pretty much the same from the outside, but inside Charlie had fixed it all up. He'd found a couple of old chairs and a table and had redone the roof so the rain stayed out. He'd hung some pieces of tarp over the window and door and it was very dark inside. I inspected his work and told him how great it was. I promised to bring over an old flashlight so we'd have light inside.

We talked about the baseball team and I told him about my grandparents' farm and what I did there. He wanted to visit it sometime. I asked him what his family meeting was about.

He stared at the ground. "N-n-n-n-n-nuthin. F-f-f-f-f-amily s-s-s-stuff."

CHAPTER Seven

When my son Livingston was born, I vowed to myself to make him comfortable playing with "girl" toys as well as those for boys. I wanted him to be free of those stereotypes which sometimes cause immense pain to people later in life. His half-sister Jordan got exposed to all kinds of opportunities, be they classic male or female interests. I had noticed, however, when she got tired or upset, she would cling to her doll or her favorite book (something called *Silly Tilly Witch*), but I just put that down to her mother's influence. Kids don't come out predisposed to any sex-related roles.

I couldn't have been more wrong.

Livingston, from the time he could hold anything, only wanted to play with balls. And trucks. And anything that shot projectiles, from guns to bows to slingshots to laser pens. The problem, I think, is not in what kids are attracted to. It is our culture's heritage to attach value to certain roles and interests. The kids aren't screwed up; our culture is. We need to equally celebrate all interests and abilities.

That said, by the time I was ten I had learned, mostly from four older brothers, that the best game guys could play was to find objects to throw, hurl, project, kick, toss, fling, pitch, lob, heave, bombard or launch at each other with the sole intent of causing the other guy pain and degradation. Because I was one of the younger boys, I learned quickly how to do it and how to fight and how to take a direct hit. To this day, the sight of a corncob makes me flinch. Those puppies sting like the devil when they hit bare skin.

There was nothing special about my brothers and I doing this. All the guys did it. We invented war games—with whatever was on hand. Snowballs, corncobs, marbles, stones, mudballs, sticks (one of my favorite war games was,   finding sticks in the woods and breaking them around a tree so the broken off end would fly and hit the other guy), pieces of corn, cow patties, rotten eggs or any fruit or vegetable we didn't like to eat. Just the Christmas before, my folks had taken us to see the movie *A Christmas Story* and all of us boys roared with laughter every time someone said to Ralphie, "You'll put your eye out" because our mom had said that to us about a gazillion times.

Actually, we had a great grandmother who got hit with a snowball and lost an eye and forever after had a piece of gauze and an eye patch which almost kept up with the ooze. When I was bad, I had to go see Grandma Borst. What a memory, 'cause she was really nice. But we all hated her.

Our fort was a natural for war games. We could play everything from cowboys and Indians to GIs and Nazis to Yankees and Rebs to cops and robbers. But my favorite was good knights versus bad knights. Our fort was the castle. Our weapons were mudballs and stick swords and the absolute best of all was something Charlie invented. He found several old style coffee cans in the barn and we stripped down small trees next to the fort and wired the cans to the trees. Pull the tree back and we had mini catapults to launch mudballs. We could fling a mudball 200 feet out to the sandbar which ran halfway 'round our island.

Because we were older, we would make Tim and Jimmie be the bad knights attacking the castle which we defended. Like with all war games, a guy wasn't "dead" until he decided he was dead. Or when he was hurt so bad he cried. Which rarely happened. They would start at the end of the sandbar and have to wade through the water and come up the hill. For Tim and Jimmie to win, they had to either "kill" us (never happened) or they had to touch the fort. Which they only did once in a great while. But when they did, we had to become the bad knights and take a turn on attack.

We had just started a war one day later in summer and Charlie and I came up with a new plan to repel the attack. Instead of each of us making up mudballs, loading and firing our own catapult, Charlie would make the mudballs and load the catapult and I would aim and fire while Charlie made the next mudball. It was a great plan. We'd fired about a dozen shots and even actually hit Tim once ("Not dead. Barely touched me!") and our timing got screwed up. I was aiming and waiting for a good shot and Charlie turned with a new mudball to load the catapult again just as I released it. It caught him full in the face, can and mudball. He went down like a rock.

I couldn't move. I just looked at him lying on the ground. Face covered with mud and then I saw blood oozing through the dirt. I thought I had killed him. Tim and Jimmie came running up the hill yelling "What happened? Is he okay?" Charlie rolled over and sat up, put his hand on his face and winced. He pulled his tee shirt off and wiped at the mess on his face. He winced again. He had a huge cut which ran from the side of his eye halfway down his cheek, the blood was still running from it. He put his shirt against it to stop the flow.

"Don't let those guys touch the fort," he commanded.

On cue, Jimmie ran over to the fort and slapped it and yelled, "We win. We win!" He jumped up and down in celebration. Only then did he walk back over to his brother and ask, "You okay?"

Charlie had not cried or whined or acted at all like he was hurt. "Yeah, I'm okay. Just a little cut. Our turn to attack the castle." He jumped up, grabbed his stick sword and started down towards the sandbar. I told him I thought he should at least wash the dirt out of the cut so when he got to the water, he splashed it over his face a couple of times. I saw him wince again and kind of shiver. When he stood up, I saw that the cut was very jagged and was still seeping blood. I told him I thought he should have his mom look at it.

He looked at me and smiled. "Nah. It's no big deal," and the blood started running again. He finally agreed to go home and get a Band-Aid. We yelled up to our brothers that we were going up to the house and they hurled insults back at us, calling us cheaters and losers and quitters. I swore they would pay for that. We all made our way back to their house.

Charlie's mom didn't seem that upset about it but wanted to know if Jimmie had done that to his brother.

"No, ma'am. It's my fault." I confessed, trying to fight back tears. I was scared she wasn't gonna let us ever come back.

"No big deal," she said and she got some antiseptic and a couple of butterfly bandages and cleaned the cut and patched him up. Charlie just sat there and said nothing but I knew it must hurt like sin. After she was done, she turned to Tim and me and said, "You boys should probably go on home now but be sure to come back tomorrow if you want. I'm sure Charlie will be ready by then to try to kill himself again." She smiled that great smile and I felt better.

Dinner at our house was called supper. Farm folk in Iowa generally ate their big meal at noon and that was dinner. It was a carryover from the days when machines didn't do all the work on the farm. The men would come in from the fields, eat three or four thousand calories, go back to the fields till dusk and then come in for a smaller meal of two thousand calories. Plus dessert. When the machines took over all the hard labor, the men just kept eating the same way. Which is why you never see a skinny farmer any more. Except my dad and grandpa. They ate well, but they had to compete with the horde of children.

At supper, we ate at a long table which was actually two picnic tables placed end to end. Grandpa had built two regular chairs which he and dad sat in at the ends of the tables and all the kids sat on benches. As best as I can remember, I don't think Mom ever sat during dinner. Funny, I never thought that odd at the time, but I wonder where she was when we ate. If she was smart, and she was, I suspect she got herself a glass of wine and hid from us. We kids took turns settin' the table, riddin' up the dishes and washin' them.

The competition for food was intense, everybody grabbing and reaching for dishes all willy-nilly. You ate fast if you wanted seconds. If you didn't like what was on the table, you heard from either Dad or Grandpa, "Fine. If you don't like it, don't eat it. Someone will." We learned not to complain. Except about liver. We were allowed to complain about that.

There was little conversation to get in the way. Which is why, when Tim loudly announced, "Cutter hit Charlie in the face with a mudball today and cut his cheek wide open. There was blood everywhere. It was really gross," everybody stopped eating. He stuffed another roll into his mouth. Which was smart 'cause I was ready to stuff my fist in his mouth. Dad's forkful of pork chop stopped halfway to his face.

"What?" he grumbled.

Mom had appeared out of nowhere. "Winston Weller Williams, what did you do?" Tim started to say something but saw the look I was giving him and backed down.

"Aw, Mom, it was nothing. We were just foolin' around and Charlie accidentally got cut." I glared at Tim to make sure he knew if he even peeped he was gonna get clobbered later. "He'll be fine. His mom put a Band-Aid on it and said it was okay."

"We'll see," she said and walked over to the wall phone and dialed a number. I prayed hard that Mrs. Settler wouldn't rat me out.

She didn't. But I still got sent to bed without dessert. and counted myself lucky.

CHAPTER EIGHT

The next day, Mom said we had to stay home and try to figure out how not to kill ourselves and each other. To make it worse, she ordered that I remain with Dad all day and help him. Which, of course, made Dad mad. He pouted. I pouted. He was doing the monthly sterilization of all the milking equipment and tubing that moved the milk from udder to milking machine to storage tank without ever being touched by air. It was a long and boring job. Mostly I just had to stand around and hand him stuff. We didn't even get to ride on the tractor or nuthin'.

"So tell me, Cutter, how did you manage to cut Charlie's face with a mud ball?"

I thought a minute and decided to come clean. Besides, I thought he might think the catapults were really smart.

He didn't. "I can't believe the ways you boys can come up with to try to hurt each other." He paused. "You think Charlie was gonna have to get stitches?" The eight Williams kids required stitches so often, we were on the group discount plan.

"His mom said 'no' but it looked pretty bad to me. It ran from here to here, " and I traced the cut on my face.

Dad's eyebrows went up and he said, "That sounds pretty serious. It must have hurt a lot."

I shook my head. "You know, Dad, it was really funny. He acted like it wasn't anything at all. He wanted to keep playing, not even get a Band-Aid or nuthin'. It's like nuthin' hurts him. He gets hit by a pitch and just smiles. He fell down the stairs and bruised the whole side of his face and head and said it hadn't hurt at all. Charlie's really tough."

"When did he fall down the stairs?"

"The last week of school. Right after we got our grades. He was out the whole week 'cause of it."

Dad didn't say anything for a long time. He kept working on the milking machines and nodding his head, like he did when he was trying to figure something out. Finally he asked, "So, do you like Charlie's parents? What are they like?"

"Oh, Mrs. Settler is great. She's really nice and makes great cookies." I decided I was sounding like a dork so I added, "I mean, she's okay for a mom."

"What about Charlie's dad?"

"I dunno. He's okay I guess. He yells sometimes, but he never talks to us kids."

"Hmmmm," was all Dad said in reply.

I finished my penance of dad chores and was washing the dishes after supper (I actually didn't mind this chore since my washing partner was always Patti and she did most of the work. All I had to do was dry and stack.) and I heard Dad asking my mom about the Settlers. I didn't hear her response.

It was almost the end of July and that meant two things: The Clinton County Fair and the little league playoffs the week after that. Since there were few dairy farmers in Clinton County, Dad and Grandpa always felt like they had to show up to prove pigs and corn weren't the only things Iowa farmers could produce. Besides, Grandpa said, there was a lot less competition for dairy blue ribbons. All I knew was, we got to go spend four days there and, even though the fairgrounds were only five miles from home, we slept in the barn with the cows.

We rolled out our sleeping bags on straw in one of the stalls next to our cows. Four of us went. John, the oldest, was 20 by then and wanted nothing to do with cows or farms. He'd had his fill of them and was working as a greenskeeper at the Springbrook Country Club. Patti, who was 19, was home from college at Iowa State and had a summer job in Davenport. Likewise, Jim, 17, worked as a lifeguard at the city pool 'cause, as he said, "someone would pay him to sit on his butt and talk to girls." Cathy Rose was 8 and she was working on her own blue ribbons doing 4H stuff. That left the cows to Tad, Chris, me and Tim.

I saved my allowance for at least a month and Grandpa always gave us twenty bucks each, but we had to buy our own food out of it. That left plenty of money for games and rides, unless you were like Tim. He went out the first day and spent all of his money trying to win a cowboy holster and gun set at some stupid ring toss game. I tried to tell him it was a fix, but he said he didn't care, he was gonna win. He didn't.

The third day we were there, I asked Dad if Charlie could spend the last night with us. He said it was okay with him if it was okay with Charlie's parents, so I called him and asked him. He said he didn't think he could 'cause they didn't have money to go to the fair, but he would ask. I told him we had a farm pass and he wouldn't need any money so his mom said okay.

It was great. Mom picked him up the next morning and, since he'd never been there, I showed him the whole fair. He liked the tractors and cows and pigs and stuff, but he really loved the midway. He stared at the Ferris wheel and asked if I'd been on it. I told him, "Sure. Lotsa times. Wanna go on it?"

"Can we? Does it cost lots?" I told him it didn't and bought us tickets. At first he seemed a little scared, but he quickly got over it. He especially liked it when, at the end of the ride, they stop and let folks off and you get to sit at the very top for a minute or so. We rode three straight times. But the thing I noticed most was when we had fair fries—you know, the really greasy ones in a big cone which taste really great and then in half an hour you feel sick, and he said they were the best thing he'd ever had to eat. It was the first time in my life I thought about being poor. And how bad it would be. I remember that whole day like it was yesterday.

Charlie loved sleeping in the cow barn. We watched the tractor pull and then stayed up really late, playing cards and walking around the grounds when it was all dark and quiet. We got up really early the last day and had corn dogs for breakfast. We dropped Charlie off late in the afternoon and my dad said to me, "Cutter, did you notice that Charlie did not stutter once the whole time he was at the fair?" I hadn't.

The following week was the most important of the summer. Little league playoffs. We finished first in the league of six teams. We'd played everyone twice and only lost one game, that to our enemies, the Redhawks. We beat them the other game and they had forfeited one game 'cause not enough players showed up one time, so they were almost as good as us. All the teams got to play in the playoffs and I don't remember how the tournament worked, but we won our first two games and then got to play the Redhawks for the championship.

Red had pitched the first game, Jerry the second and Charlie was to pitch the final game. We all talked about where we were gonna put the trophies we won. Mine was gonna go on the living room mantel. We started out real strong. We scored three runs in the first inning and Charlie was mowing them down. By the third inning we were leading 3 to 1 and Charlie struck out the side. He was throwing so hard my hand was aching.

In the fourth inning, it fell apart. Charlie couldn't find the plate. He gave up three walks and then a double and suddenly they were ahead 4 to 3. He walked another batter, then another and had filled the bases. Coach Weaver called time out and went to talk with Charlie. Charlie told him his arm hurt and he couldn't throw straight. The coach called Red in to take over. Charlie took her place in the outfield.

Red warmed up for about five throws and the ump called "Play ball." Before Red could make her first pitch, the other coach called time and walked over to the ump. They talked, then the ump talked to Coach Weaver. Because of the rules of little league, a player couldn't pitch with less than four day's rest. Because it was a tournament, Red had pitched just three days before. The only thing to do was bring in someone new (please, Coach, not me) or have Charlie keep pitching. When the ump announced what was happening, there were boos from the fans.

Coach asked Charlie if he could still do it. Charlie smiled and said, "I'll sure try, Coach." In 1997, I watched The Flu Game, arguably the greatest performance of Michael Jordan's illustrious career. That performance paled compared to what Charlie did the rest of that game. He was never better. He had never thrown harder. Over the final 2⅔ innings, he gave up no hits, one walk and no runs. We lost 4 to 3.

After the game was over, we lined up and walked past the Redhawk players with the obligatory "Good game, good game, good game," as we shook hands. The coach gathered us around the bench and started to tell us what a great job we did and what good kids we were and all that crappola. The Redhawk coach came over and just as he started to talk, the crowd got very quiet so everyone heard him say, "Thanks, Weaver, for making me look like an asshole on that pitcher deal."

Red's dad yelled down from the stands, "You didn't need his help." Everyone laughed, except Charlie. He was too busy blaming himself for the loss. No one else did.

CHAPTER NINE

Summer, just like that, was over. Fifth grade. Two weeks before school started, we made the annual trek to the NorthPark Mall in Davenport. Hundreds of stores to shop in for school clothes, though we always actually bought them at Sears or JC Penney. You'd think, what with having all those older brothers, all I would get to wear would be hand me downs. Truth be told, with four older brothers, clothes were pretty much worn to shreds before they got to me, so I got to pick out five of everything for school. Five pairs of pants, which were always jeans, not real jeans like Levi's, but Roebucks, Sears' rip off copies of real jeans. Five shirts, a five-pack of tee shirts, tighty whities and socks. A new pair of sneakers. No Adidas or Nike or anything like that. Nope. Sears canvas sneakers. The smell on the first day of school was always new clothes.

Mrs. Settler called my mom and invited Tim and me to Charlie's birthday party on Labor Day, right before school started. Mom took us to the store to buy him a gift. We got him a Mr. T tee shirt on accounta he loved *The A-Team* on television. On the front it said, "I pity the fool." His party was just his mom and brothers and sisters and Tim and me. His dad wasn't there. We had hamburgers and potato chips and birthday cake. It was the most unfancy and funnest birthday party ever because after the cake and after he opened our gift, he got a gift from his family. They had all gone together and saved whatever they could and bought Charlie his first ever new baseball glove—a Rawlings Ricky Henderson model. I don't have to tell you, you just don't get better than Rawlings.

Charlie was more excited than I had ever seen him. "G-g-g-g-g-gosh, g-g-g-g-guys. Th-th-thanks." I had never heard him stutter around his family. They were all hugging each other and Woody, his oldest brother, started telling him about how to break in the glove and how to take care of it and why it was such a good glove. Everybody seemed to be as excited about that baseball glove as Charlie was. All of us went outside afterwards and played catch for a long time—all seven of his family, including his mom. It was the best game of catch I ever played. It just made me so darned happy seeing them all that happy and excited about a baseball glove.

The first day of school always made me a little nervous. Everybody walking around in stiff jeans and new shirts and dress up dresses. You had to check out the new kids and see if anyone had left. Two of the squad had moved, Fat Jimmy and Dave the Brain. Somebody said Dave's dad had gotten a job in Chicago, but nobody knew what happened to Fat Jimmy and his family. They had a small farm and apparently the sheriff came and made them leave 'cause of taxes or something. By the time you're in fifth grade and one of the big kids in school, you get used to people leaving. Still, we felt kinda bad about the squad not being together for the first time since first grade.

There was also this new girl who had orange hair and freckles and was kinda cute, I guess. She wore a really fancy blue dress and her long hair had a ribbon in it. And she walks right up to me. I'm a little surprised this new girl was gonna talk to me. She gets real close, hits me on the shoulder, hard, and says, "Cutter, it's me. Red. What's wrong with you? Acting like you don't know me." And she punches me again in the shoulder. I couldn't believe it. Where were the jeans and dirty tee shirt and sneakers and the ball cap she always stuffed her hair up into? Geez, she's a girl. But it seemed okay. I guess.

We were supposed to have a nun as a teacher, but instead we had this man teacher, Mr. Turner. We'd never had a male teacher so it was a little scary, but the very first day, after he wrote his name on the board, he asked us a question. "Why do they have fences around cemeteries?"

Several of the suck-ups' hands went into the air. Like Booger Conners. Trying to show the teacher how smart they were and all. Mr. Turner pointed at Booger who said, very seriously, "So no one steals the dead people?"

"Nope. You," and he pointed at Betty.

"To protect the headstones?" she guessed.

"Nope." The other hands which had been waving in the air had all disappeared. "Give up?" We all nodded our heads.

"Because," he said, all serious like, "Because people are just dyin' to get in." And he laughed, real loud. About half the class laughed with him. The other half just looked confused. A teacher telling jokes? They're not supposed to do that. Are they? I decided right then and there it was gonna be the best school year ever.

He then pointed at Charlie, who was sitting behind me. "You, young man, would you mind standing for a minute?" Charlie stood up, head kinda hanging down and his face reddening. "What's your name?"

Face full on red now. "Ch-ch-ch-ch-ch-ch-arlie." A couple of kids snickered. Mr.Turner's face also got red and he looked a little scary.

"Listen. All of you." Mr. Turner's voice was low and quiet, but it sounded like yelling. "When someone has an issue like stuttering, like my friend Charlie here, it is nothing to laugh about or make fun of.

We all have problems and the only way we are going to get through this year is if we all help each other be better people. Understand?" Lots of red faces now and lots of heads nodding. "Charlie, come up here for a minute if you don't mind."

Charlie walked to the front of the room. His head was not hanging and he wasn't exactly smiling, but I knew he was feeling pretty good. When he got to the front, Mr. Turner stood behind him and put his hands on Charlie's shoulders. I hadn't realized until then how tall Mr. Turner was. Which was very. He had huge hands and was real thin. He looked a little like pictures of Abe Lincoln. Before the beard.

He continued, "So, today Charlie is going to teach the class. Right, Charlie?"

Charlie actually smiled, the first time ever in the classroom. "Yessir." No stutter.

"Great. So what are we going to teach? Reading? Arithmetic? Science?"

Charlie thought for a minute and said, "W-w-w-we could teach everyone how to do batting averages. That's arithmetic, right?"

Mr. Turner smiled. "That's a great idea." He handed Charlie some chalk and Charlie went to the board and started showing us how to do batting averages. He stuttered a couple of times and Mr. Turner told him when he started to stutter to just stop, think about what he was going to say, then start again when he was ready. He pointed to the rest of the class and said, "You can see, they're not going anywhere until you finish and you can take all the time you want." Now Charlie grinned. We all learned how to do batting averages.

Finally Red piped up and asked, "So if a guy bats a bunch of times and doesn't get even one hit, what's his average?" Charlie put up the figures for dividing zero by ten. He pondered it for a minute until Mr. Turner came to his rescue.

"His batting average would be .000. Zero divided by any number is always zero." More nodding heads.

Red grinned and announced, "Well, that's what any player batting against Charlie would get." Everybody laughed.

"Charlie, do you know why I asked you to stand up?" Mr. Turner asked. Charlie shook his head. "Because of your tee shirt. I also pity the fool." Made me kinda proud to have given it to Charlie. He patted Charlie on the shoulder and told him to take his seat.

Mr. Turner was one of the best teachers I ever had. We didn't just learn book stuff. He talked about everything. He knew sports and he talked about farming and how important it was. He told us about places he'd been and things he'd done, like being in the Vietnam War. He wouldn't tell us what he did there, but about what the country and people were like. At recess he would even come out and play softball with us. But most important, he was fair to Charlie.

Charlie's stuttering got less and less. He spoke up in class. I was pretty used to being one of the smart kids and with Dave the Brain gone, maybe the smartest in the class. That is, until Mr. Turner worked with Charlie. It seemed like he beat me on every test. The week before Thanksgiving we had a big spelling bee. Spelling was my best subject so I was sure I was gonna win. I didn't. Charlie and I were the last two contestants. I got the word "pneumonia" and spelled it exactly right. Except for the "p".

Charlie got it right and won. I got really mad at him. He was supposed to be my friend.

I didn't see him over the entire Thanksgiving break which was fine with me. When we got back to school the next week, Charlie was stuttering again. Bad.

CHAPTER TEN

The Monday after Thanksgiving I got on the bus and saw Charlie in the back seat sitting between Jimmie and Carol. He normally saved me a seat but it was okay 'cause I was still a little torqued at him. He kinda nodded his head at me when I got on the bus and I nodded back but we didn't talk, even when we got to the classroom. We had started out the year sitting next to each other but Mr. Turner had moved Charlie to the front early on. He had moved Red to the seat behind me.

We started the day, as we always did, with religion class. Mr. Turner told us he liked to have religion first because that's when we were most alert and it was the most important class. We knew that was bull hockey. He just liked to get it outta the way before we woke up. At the end of the lesson he reminded us that Advent would start the week after next. Which meant Christmas was almost here. That woke us up.

We spent the next period in reading class where we were reading *The Phantom Tollbooth*. We would take turns reading out loud for about half the class then read to ourselves for the rest of it. Mr. Turner would skip around the class asking people to read so you never knew when you were gonna be called. After Sweet Willie struggled through several paragraphs, Mr. Turner called on Charlie. We were at the part where Milo and Tock were in Dictionopolis.

Charlie started, "I-I-I-I-I-I-I n-n-n-n-n-n-n-ev-ev-er kn-n-n-n-n-n-new." He stopped and took a deep breath and started again. "I-I-I n-n-n-n-n-n...." Mr. Turner had moved to Charlie's desk and put a hand on his shoulder.

"That's good, Charlie. Andy, why don't you start there?" Andy started reading and Mr. Turner continued to stand by Charlie, now with both hands on his shoulders. We finished reading class and were dismissed for recess. What was left of the squad played touch football with some of the dweebs. Except for Red, who had started wearing dresses to school and wouldn't play sports. Good thing, too, since she thought all football was tackle and she hit hard. Charlie didn't play either. He had to stay in and talk to Mr. Turner.

When we returned to class, Charlie was not there. Mr. Turner said he was not feeling well and had gone to the nurse's office. He was not on the bus that afternoon, nor was he at school on Tuesday or Wednesday. Wednesday after school I tried calling but a message said the phone had been disconnected. Even though it was cold, windy and spitting rain, I rode my bike through the woods to see him.

No one was outside and I knocked on the door. Mrs. Settler answered and asked me to come in. Charlie was sitting at the kitchen table studying spelling. "Hey," was all I said.

"Hey, C-c-c-c-cutter, whatcha doin' here?" He didn't look sick to me.

"Nuthin. I didn't have nuthin to do so I thought I'd take a bike ride. Just stopped in to see if you're comin' back to school sometime."

He smiled. "Nice day for a bike ride. Wish I'd thought of that." No stutter this time. "I'll be back tomorrow. Spelling test, you know, and I gotta kick your butt again." He laughed. He was back to being Charlie. It made me feel better.

The next day Charlie saved me a seat on the bus and things were back to normal. We spent the bus ride drilling each other on spelling words and talking about Christmas. Everybody in class kinda waited to see how Charlie was and when he didn't stutter, they all relaxed. After we had our spelling test, Mr. Turner released us for recess but since it was about 30 degrees outside, we had recess in the classroom.

Charlie, Red and I had just started a game of Chinese checkers when Mr. Turner came back and asked Charlie to go to the office with him. That's normally the kind of thing that would really get to Charlie but today he jumped up and said "Sure," and followed the teacher out of the room. He was back in about three minutes.

"You in trouble?" Red asked.

"Nah. It's nuthin."

"Why d'ja have to go to Sister Mary Magdaline's office?" I was interested now.

"Mr. Turner just wanted to know if some people from the county came to see my folks." He didn't elaborate.

"Why the county?" Red and I were in full nosy mode.

"I dunno."

"Well, did they?" Red demanded.

"I guess. Some people in a white car came a couple of days ago, but my dad run 'em off. Told 'em to get the heck off our property. It was funny. They lit out like they were on fire. I just told Mr. Turner they came and left right away." He paused and bounced his head up and down like he was thinking about something. "So, let's start the game again." We did.

The next four weeks dragged on and on and on. It was always like that between Thanksgiving and Christmas. I mean, there was lots of fun stuff, but it seemed like Christmas would never, ever get here. We got to sing lots of Christmas hymns and songs in music class, we made decorations for the little class Christmas tree and drew names for a gift exchange. I traded to get Charlie's and Booger told me that Red had traded him to get my name. Nobody wanted a girl to get your name, but I figured since it was Red, it'd be okay.

Two weeks before Christmas, the whole family, including Grandpa, piled into the van and drove down to Davenport to go shopping and see the decorations at the mall and to visit Santa. Only Cathy Rose, Tim and I actually sat on his lap and I didn't really believe, but, you know, this close to the big day, you couldn't take any chances. Cathy Rose still believed and I think so did Tim. Funny thing is, even to this day, I feel the same way about Santa. If I have any religion, that's it.

Because I had Charlie's name at school, Tim wanted to buy Jimmie a present as well, which led us to wanting to get something for Carol too. I got Charlie a new baseball, which is more than we were supposed to spend, but I'd just tell them I got it on sale. We got some board game for Carol and I can't remember what Tim got for Jimmie. Afterwards we had dinner and then drove through the neighborhoods looking at Christmas lights.

A few days later, Mom said that Mrs. Settler had called and asked us not to bring any gifts to her kids, on accounta they didn't have much money and couldn't get us anything. I told Mom I had to give him mine since it was for class. Dad said that was okay but we should respect her request for the rest of them. Then he and Mom got into a discussion and Mom came up with a plan to take them a big basket with food and stuff and hide the presents in it and they would take it over without us and tell Mrs. Settler it was a thank you gift for all the times they let Tim and me hang out there and for feeding us and all. Dad smiled and said okay to that plan. Mom pretty much always won those discussions.

The last day of school was the Friday before Christmas which meant we still had to go another whole four days until the big day itself. We had our morning religion class, then Mr. Turner let us just play until the home room moms showed up after lunch for our class party. The party was fine, lots of cookies to eat and we sang a bunch of Christmas songs and then the priest came in and kinda tried to ruin it all by telling us to remember about Jesus and all, but then we got to open presents. Charlie loved the baseball and first asked all the guys on the team to sign it and then decided to have everyone in the class sign it, including Mr. Turner. He said he was never ever gonna play with it on accounta it being brand new and all.

I got this kinda big present to open and it was a Ryne Sandberg jersey. Ryne was like the best player on the Cubs team and he was my favorite, even though he played second base and I was a catcher. Anyway, it was really neat and I knew it cost lots more than we were supposed to spend but I still loved it. There was a card in it with Red's real name, Lynne, on it and a heart. I was looking at it, trying to decide what that meant when Sweet Willie's mom, who was a home room mom, looked over my shoulder and said, "Oh, Cutter, I think somebody has a crush on you."

I shook my head and started to tell her "no way" but I just turned red and said nothing. I told Red, "Thanks," and chucked her on the shoulder so she wouldn't get the wrong idea. It made me feel funny. Good, but funny. I watched her when she didn't know I was looking and thought about how she was a girl and all. I had to admit I kinda liked that.

The last few days before Christmas were agony. Wait. Wait. Wait some more. Then wait. Finally, it was Christmas Eve and we had a big dinner and lots of cookies and eggnog and candy and disgusting fruitcake, and then we all went to midnight Mass. I had asked Santa for a new basketball. The old one was all lopsided and stuff and bounced funny. I really wanted a leather one but that was way too expensive so I'd be happy with one that was round.

The next morning we opened presents. In the Williams' house that takes a long, long time. With eight kids and two parents and Grandpa Weller and with us having to watch each and every present opened it took like three hours. But I got my new basketball, not leather, but real nice and after all the presents were opened and all the coffee cake eaten and before we packed up to go to the Williams grandparents' house, my mom pulled me aside.

"Win, your dad has one more present for you." Now the whole family was around me. "It's in the barn." We all trooped out there and I followed dad up to the haymow. We had a basketball hoop up there, nailed to the wall. And there it was. The best present I ever got, except maybe when the universe gave me Jordan, Livingston and Rachel. My dad had replaced the old basket with a new one on a real backboard and best of all, he had nailed all of the floor boards down and sanded them smooth so we had a real court to play on. He'd even painted a foul line. It was amazing. Everybody applauded and we took turns shooting the new ball until mom made us load up for Christmas, round two.

CHAPTER ELEVEN

The problem with winter is that it drags on forever. Sure, you want cold and snow for Christmas, even New Year's Eve. But then it just hangs around and makes a royal pain of itself. Day in and day out, cold, snow, gray. You're in your house, in school or on the bus. You try to go outside and the fun lasts like, two minutes. The new basketball court was great, but you know they don't heat those barns and even there it got too cold to play. On the warmest days, Charlie and Jimmie and Tim and I would play b-ball from after school until dinner. Sometimes some of my older brothers and sisters would join in and a couple of times Charlie's older brothers came over. Since it was my ball and my court, I got to be Michael Jordan. Charlie always wanted to be Larry Bird.

Turned out Charlie was a pretty fair basketball player as well. Also, he seemed to be growing. When he first came to our school, I thought he was littler than me. By spring, he was a good three inches taller than I was. Which meant he would often cram my shot back into my face. So I made him my teammate as often as I could. He was the kind of guy who would rather pass you the ball than take an open shot himself. Which I liked, since mostly I just like shooting. Lots of fouls got called on accounta our having a foul line to shoot from, though I noticed guys would hack Charlie or shove him or whatever and he never called a foul. My brother Chris elbowed him once and bloodied his nose and Charlie just wiped it away and kept playing.

By the end of March, we were so done with basketball and ready for our favorite sport, baseball. Charlie and I would practice outside if it got over 45 degrees, in the hay mow if it didn't. He spent hours trying to get the hang of a curve ball and by the time the season finally arrived, he had a whole new weapon to throw from the mound. Truth be told, though, he threw so much harder than he had the year before no one was gonna be able to hit his fastball anyway.

By spring, which seemed slow in arriving, we had all settled into a familiar routine. School and baseball or softball, as little farm work as we could get away with and back to our adventures in the woods. Charlie and Jimmie and Tiny Tim and I spent most of our days and evenings together. We were a well-oiled play machine. And we were itching to get back on the official baseball diamond—this was gonna be our year.

In mid-May, I got on the bus one morning and Charlie wasn't there. Carol and Jimmie were and I asked them if Charlie was sick. Carol told me what had happened. The night before, after I got off the bus, Charlie had gotten into a fight and got kicked off the bus for the rest of the school year. Carol was almost crying when she told me.

"I was singing with my friend Penny and that Wanda Folk girl yelled at us to shut up." Wanda was a high school girl who sometimes rode our bus when her ride didn't pick her up. Her younger brother Jeff was in my brother Chris' class and he was a full time bully and jerk. Things he obviously learned from his sister. Carol went on, "Anyway, we kept singing and Wanda grabbed my shirt and pulled me into the aisle and pushed me down. Charlie jumped up and pushed her back and she punched Charlie right in the face. Then the stupid bus driver stopped the bus and started yelling at all of us and Wanda lied and told him that Charlie had hit her and when we got home, the bus driver told Charlie he wasn't allowed back on the bus this year. We tried to tell him it was Wanda who started it, but he wouldn't listen. And then, stupid Wanda stuck her tongue out at us as we got off the bus. I hate her."

I looked at Jimmie who only said, "I'm gonna get her somehow." He sounded like he meant it. Wanda had become our mutual enemy.

"So how's Charlie gonna get to school?"

Carol answered, "Dad's gonna bring him. But he got real mad at Charlie and he wouldn't listen when we told him it wasn't Charlie's fault and he said he didn't care and told us all to shut up or else. Then he told Charlie that he wasn't gonna get to play baseball this summer. And that he better learn to behave himself or they would send him away."

That kinda stunned us all into silence. Charlie might get "sent away"? He might not get to play little league? What could we do? It was Wanda's fault and nobody had believed Charlie or Jimmie or Carol, so why would they believe me or Tim? This just didn't feel fair.

Charlie was at school, at his desk, when we got there. He told us pretty much what Carol had said but added, "No big deal. I'm sure Dad will let me play." I told him he should tell Mr. Turner to see if he could get Charlie back on the bus. Maybe then his dad wouldn't be so mad. Mr. Turner said he would try, but he couldn't get the stupid bus driver to change his mind either.

That night we were watching *The A-Team* on TV and it made me start thinking about Charlie and I wasn't really paying attention and Mom asked me what was wrong. Mom was pretty good about figuring out when something was wrong, especially when you didn't really want to talk about it, so I told her, "Nuthin." Course that didn't stop big mouth Tim from telling her about how Charlie had been kicked off the bus and how it wasn't fair and all. Mom asked me if I wanted her to talk to Mrs. Settler.

"I don't know. I don't want Charlie to get into any more trouble, but we really need him on the team and he was cheated." She said she would talk to our father and they'd think about it. Two days later, as we were eating breakfast, Dad came in from the barn.

"Alright you three, hurry up and get in the car. The bus is leaving in two minutes." The three of us were me and Tim and Cathy Rose.

Cathy Rose looked confused and said, "But Daddy, the bus doesn't get here for another ten minutes."

"Well, I'm your new bus driver and my bus leaves in one minute." We didn't really understand but grabbed our backpacks and loaded up. When we got out to the end of our road, we turned right instead of left towards town.

"Where we goin'?"

"You'll see."

We turned down Settler's lane and Charlie, Jimmie and Carol were all standing on their porch waiting for us. They loaded up and Dad turned and told us, "Okay guys, I'm gonna be your bus driver through the end of the year. Your moms worked this out so that Charlie could play ball. And because it didn't seem right what was happening on that bus. We're going to talk with the principal later, but for now, I'm it." He faced the front and then paused and looked directly at me in the mirror. "And I'm expecting you to help out a little more in the barns." But he smiled.

Although as soon as that disaster was averted, another one struck.

Two days later, I got back into the classroom after playing softball. I was still a softball captain, but Charlie had become the other one since Red had decided she preferred dresses and dolls to our games. On my desk was a folded up note. It read:

> Do you like me?
>
> [ ] YES   [ ] NO
>
> Why? _____
>
> Fill in the blank.
>
>   Lynne

You gotta understand. Even though I was only eleven, I had figured out this whole boy/girl thing. I knew the answer was "YES." Of course, I liked her. And I knew why. Though telling her why may have been a small error in judgement. I wrote, "Because, except for Charlie, you're the best baseball player ever. Especially for a girl." I folded up the note and put it back on her desk before she got back from recess. Big smile on my face.

Red sat down just as the bell rang. She was real quiet as Mr. Turner started Social Studies. All of a sudden Mr. Turner looked in her direction and said, "Yes, Lynne?"

"I feel sick. May I go to the nurse's office?"

"Yes, certainly."

I heard her get up and half turned to look at her. She collected her books under her arm and as she walked by, she hit me in the back of the head and hissed, "I hate you."

That night, after John had gone to sleep (he and I and Jim shared a room), I worked up the nerve to ask Jim about Lynne, knowing full well he would probably give me a bunch of crap about it. "So this thing happened at school today and I think I may have screwed up. But I don't know how."

"Hey, little brother, don't be telling me anything I have to report to the 'rents."

"No, nuthin like that. It's about a girl," knowing full well this is where the crap would start. Jim just raised his eyebrows, so I told him what had happened with Red.

"Cutter, has she ever done anything like that before?"

"Well, this year she hasn't wanted to play sports and she's been wearing dresses and hanging out with the frilly girls and there was this thing where she gave me a Ryne Sandberg jersey and…" He interrupted me.

71

"Wait. That really cool jersey you have came from her?"

"Well, yeah and the gift tag had a heart on it and she signed it 'Lynne' not 'Red'."

Jim broke out laughing loud enough that John woke up and told us to shut our pie holes. Jim stood and wiggled a finger at me and motioned for me to follow him. We went to the kitchen. He broke into mom's hidden stash of Oreos and I got the milk out of the fridge. We munched cookies for a few minutes before Jim spoke again.

"You're right, Cutter, you did screw up. But it's probably fixable. Your friend Red figured out she's a girl. She knows you think she's a great ball player. But she needs to know you think she's a great girl too. So here's what we'll do. Tomorrow morning, ask Mom if she'll cut you some flowers from her garden to take to Red at school. Get there early, leave them on her desk with a note that just says 'I'm sorry'. Then hope for the best." He grabbed the last three Oreos and stuffed them in his mouth.

Jim seemed to know a lot about girls so I took his advice. When Rachel read this she pointed out that Jim has been married three times so I was probably putting my faith in the wrong person. Still, I did what he suggested. My mom and dad were grinning but helpful, and when Lynne (not Red) got to her desk, I heard her gasp a little. At lunch I saw she had written LP+WW on her notebook.

CHAPTER TWELVE

Coach Weaver called our house and asked if Tim and I wanted to come to some earlier little league practices. Tim hadn't officially tried out yet—that wouldn't happen for another three weeks—but we were itching to get to it so we were all in. I got a call from Charlie saying they'd been asked to attend as well but could only go if we could give them a ride. We'd lost four players, including one of our pitchers, so the coach was eager to figure out how to replace him. Not to mention, he'd gotten a call from Red's dad who said he didn't think Red would be playing this year. Our dreams of a championship started to fade.

When we got to practice, Coach sat us all down and said, "Okay, guys, I got some good news this morning." I figured Red had changed her mind and was gonna play. He went on, "I got a call from the coach over in the Babe Ruth league last night," he paused and pointed to Charlie, "and they want Charlie to join them this year. He'd be the youngest player ever in their league. The high school coach is already talking about Charlie being the best pitcher he's ever seen." Poof, the championship was gone, just like that. Not to mention my best friend on the team. And they hadn't even seen Charlie's curve ball yet.

"So Charlie, what do you say? You think you're ready for the big leagues?"

Charlie grinned and then looked at me. I was not grinning. I was, in fact, frowning. Charlie asked, "Can Cutter go with me?"

The coach shook his head. "I don't think so. Cutter's good, but I bet their coaches won't think he's ready yet."

Charlie looked at the coach, then at me, then at the rest of the players. No one was smiling, except the coach. "What d'ya think, Cutter?"

"I think you should do it. Since Red is gone, we're gonna be a good pitcher short anyway. Yeah, you should do it. You're ready." It made me feel a little better that he had asked me. But not much.

Charlie grinned again and turned to Coach Weaver. "Coach, c-c-c-call Red and t-t-t-tell her that if she'll come back, I'll stay so we can win the championship." The coach smiled and nodded his head. He got up and left, telling us to play catch 'til he got back. He returned in about ten minutes. "She'll play. But we have to call her Lynne from now on." We all cheered. This was gonna be our year.

We got in four practices before the official tryouts and then had our who's-gonna-play-what-position practice. Turned out that none of the new kids could hit the broad side of a barn pitching. The one kid who could throw hard kept throwing it over the backstop. We were still short a pitcher. At the end of the practice, Coach waved me over to the bench where he was sitting with Charlie. "Okay, Cutter, Charlie and I have decided. You're gonna be our third pitcher."

I started to shake my head "no" but Charlie said, "C'mon Cutter, it'll be great and I'll be your catcher. We'll be a big league b-b-b-b-battery."

We had finished the school year. I finished second in the class. Charlie finished first. I was officially Lynne's boyfriend and had to sit with her at lunch, though I got to play softball at recesses. The planting had all gotten done and brother Jim graduated from high school and three days later joined the army. Mom was not happy. Dad pointed out that it wasn't like he was going to go to war and that besides, "Maybe the army will actually teach him what it is to do real work." Still, Mom and Patti both cried when he left. Cathy Rose cried as well but only because Mom was crying.

Charlie pitched the first game and had a no hitter. No one was surprised, though he did give up a few walks trying out his curveball. He struck out 13. I had three hits, my best ever at the plate. Yep, we're gonna win the championship. Lynne pitched the next game and won. I pitched the third and gave up 11 runs, but somehow we still managed to win.

We went to pick up the Settlers for the fourth game and when they walked out, Charlie's right arm was in a cast from hand to shoulder. They got in the car. Dad said nothing.

"What's wrong with your arm?" Tim was the first to ask.

"Broke it."

"How?"

"Fell off my bike."

"When?"

"Last night. Had to go to the hospital to have it fixed."

I finally found my voice. "How are you gonna be able to pitch?"

"Can't. Doctor says I'm out for the season." Tears formed in his eyes.

"Man, that sucks." We rode the rest of the way in silence. Lynne pitched, we won, but no one on the team was happy.

The next game was a disaster. I pitched, but with Charlie out, Randy had to take over the catching duties. And as soon as they found out he couldn't throw a peg to second, everyone who got to first stole second and sometimes third. And I let lots of batters get to first. We got shellacked.

A week later, Tim and I and Charlie and Jimmie were down in the woods behind their house messing around in the creek when Mrs. Settler came towards us. "Cutter and Timmy, your mom called and said you are to come home right away. But not to worry, nothing's wrong. She sounded pretty serious so I told her I'd come get you." We trotted back to her house, grabbed our bikes and made it home in ten minutes.

When we got back to our house, there was a sheriff's car sitting in the driveway. I threw down my bike and hurdled the steps up to the porch where Dad was waiting for me. "Slow down, big guy. Nothing's wrong."

"Why is the sheriff here?" I demanded.

"He'd like to talk with you and Tim," Dad explained. "Go inside, wash up, then go into the living room and introduce yourself. Both of you." He paused. "And, Cutter, only tell the truth."

"Yessir," we answered together.

We got to the living room, hands and faces washed, and the deputy stood up as we came in. "Gentlemen, I'm Tom Reinan. I'm a deputy sheriff here in Clinton County. I'd like to talk to you each for a couple of minutes. Your folks say it's okay and they will stay here while we talk. But I do need to talk to you individually. Winston, would you mind waiting upstairs for a few minutes while I chat with Timothy?" Winston? Timothy? What was going on here? Dad nodded so I did as told. Five minutes later Dad came and got me.

"Winston, you're friends with Charles Settler, right?"

"Yessir."

"Do you know his parents?"

"Yessir. Mrs. Settler is very nice. I have never talked to their dad."

"Do you know if they ever hit Charles or any of his brothers or sisters?"

What? I thought a minute. "No sir. Not that I know of." I waited and when he didn't say anything I volunteered, "Sometimes their dad yells at them and he has lots of rules. But I don't think he hits them." The sheriff made a note on his pad. No one said anything so I just stood there and shuffled my feet.

Finally, the deputy smiled and said, "Thank you for your help, Winston. You can go now. I need to chat with your folks for a few more minutes. And, Winston, I'd appreciate it if you didn't share what I asked with any of the Settlers, okay?"

"Yessir." I went up the stairs but hung around the top to hear what else was said. I didn't get all of it but the deputy said something about "hard to

76

believe a bike accident could cause that injury." Obviously he never had a bike accident. Breaking an arm happened to lots of guys who rode bikes. It was the price you paid for not being stuck at home all the time.

Of course, within two days I had forgotten I wasn't supposed to share what he asked me. We were hanging out in the barn, looking at a *Playboy* magazine I had found in Jim's stuff after he left, and Jimmie told me, "Man if our dad found out we had this magazine, he'd beat our butts."

We all laughed but then I asked, "So does your dad beat your butts lots?"

Charlie said, "Nah. He just mostly yells at us."

Jimmie chimed in, "Sometimes he hits Charlie, but he just yells at the rest of us. One time he used his belt to give Woody a whippin' but that was a long time ago."

"Why does he hit Charlie?"

"Mom says it's on accounta Charlie looks different than the rest of us." Before anyone could react he went on, "Hey, guys, look at this picture. Wowee, that girl really has some hooters!" Jimmie pointed at the centerfold and we all howled with laughter. We were on to more important things.

CHAPTER THIRTEEN

Just in time for the last couple of weeks of baseball (and in time for the playoffs), Charlie went in to have his cast removed. We were all pretty excited about it, since it meant that we still had a chance to win the championship. Coach Weaver warned us that Charlie may still not be able to pitch and that he had to do whatever the doctor told him to do. Still, we knew that the fates were with us, that this was our year.

Tim and I rode over to Settler's the afternoon after he'd been to the doctor's. Charlie was sitting on the front porch, hunched over. As we pulled up, he waved at us with his pitching hand—which was still covered in a cast, though it was a new one.

"What happened?" I asked.

"Doctor said my arm didn't heal right. After they took the cast off, they took some x-rays and then gave me a shot of something that made my arm numb. Then they rebroke my arm. Man did that hurt. Now I gotta wear this cast for maybe ten weeks."

I told him, "Too bad," but all I could think about was that twice in one season our championship was ruined. I was right. We lost both of our games and were out of the tournament. Lynne said she was never gonna play again. I felt the same way, though I didn't say it.

The end of summer rolled into fall. We went back to school and, once again, had Mr. Turner for teacher which was okay with me. The weather grew colder, we played touch football and Lynne told me, right before we were supposed to go trick or treating, that she was no longer my girlfriend and she was now going with Randy Dunlap. She used to hate Randy. She was all the time punching him and stuff. But I guess they both liked that. I didn't really care except I guess you were supposed to have a girlfriend in sixth grade and I didn't have one.

Charlie got his cast off in November and he said it felt fine, but his arm didn't look right. It was skinny and the skin was white and flaky, which went away, but there was a hump in it near his elbow. That didn't go away. It didn't seem to affect his shooting a basketball, but when we played catch in the haymow, he couldn't throw hard and he wasn't as accurate as he used to be. After a while, he said to just forget it and promised he'd be better in time for next season.

We went through Thanksgiving and Christmas and all of crappy January and February and it was still snowing in March when I had my twelfth birthday. With Patti being away at school and Jim in the army, the house stayed kinda quiet. We hung out a lot with Jimmie and Charlie but absolutely nothing exciting happened, except, of course, that I was getting hair under my arms (and other places) and my voice was cracking and Tim kept making fun of me until I punched him in the nose and got blood all over Mom's couch and I got grounded for two weeks.

In early April, Mrs. Kenney, who worked in the principal's office, came to our classroom and told me to get my books and coat and come with her. It was bad if you got sent to the principal's office. It was worse if you got called there. But the absolute worst was if you got called there and you had to take your stuff with you.

My mom was sitting in the principal's office and Tim and Cathy Rose were already with her. Cathy Rose was crying. "What's wrong?" I tried to keep the fear out of my voice, but fear and a cracking voice just go together.

Mom said, "Cutter, your grandfather died this morning."

"What? How? What happened?"

"We don't know for sure. We think it was a heart attack. Your dad had just turned the cows out from the morning milking and was walking out through

79

the loafing shed and found him sitting, leaned up against a bale of hay. He was gone. The funeral home came to get him and we're going home now and get ready for the funeral." Tears ran down her cheek. I guess I had never really thought about it. Grandpa Weller was my grandfather, but he was also my mom's dad. Mom's dad had just died. I know how I would have felt if my dad had died and I couldn't help myself, I started bawling like a big baby. Mom gave me a big hug and, like a broody hen, she slowly moved us out and into the van.

The next few days were kind of a fog. People coming and going. Food showing up on our doorstep as if by magic. Lots of desserts which I liked. Jim and Patti came home and my uncles, Mom's brothers, and their wives came back to the farm. After a couple of days, I would forget about Grandpa dying and then it would come back to me and I would feel bad all over again. The funeral was at the church and like everyone in town showed up. I could tell it made my mom feel good but also made her even sadder, if that makes any sense.

What happened next, I don't really remember but will tell you what my parents explained to us later. For us kids, life went on more or less the same until the next fall. Then our lives turned pretty much upside down.

Summer was a bust. With Grandpa gone, all of us had to do more work on the farm. Charlie and Jimmie would come over and help us with our chores so we got to mess around some, just not as much as we had. Dad always seemed grumpy and Mom always seemed sad. Our last year of Little League was a total failure. Charlie never got back the strength in his pitching arm and he played first base most of the season. Red didn't play and the new kids on the team were all geeks and nerds. It just wasn't fun anymore.

We did spend a lot of time at the Dewitt Municipal Swimming Pool, mostly showing off for the girls and trying to get crotch shots by swimming around the girls who sat on the side of the pool. When we weren't doing that, we played the video games they had there. Lots of Super Mario Brothers and Outrun, which was like the coolest game of the year. Every quarter I had went into those games. Except for the ones that bought Cokes and chips.

Early in August, Mom ordered us to all be home by four o'clock so we could get cleaned up 'cause she and Dad were taking us to like the best restaurant ever—Bishop's Buffet in Davenport. It was a buffet and you could eat all you wanted, including desserts. Cathy Rose loved the banana pudding. It was okay, but I liked the chocolate cream pie best. Mom would make us eat something real first, but I was always able to save room for like three or four pieces of pie and still have some ice cream. It was awesome.

After we finished dinner, we hopped back in the van and instead of heading home, we drove to a place called the East Village and started driving around the neighborhood. Chris finally asked where we were going. Mom smiled and said, "You'll see. It's just a couple more minutes."

We pulled up behind a car parked at the corner of Fulton and Ridgewood and Dad parked and got out and started talking to the guy in the car. After a couple of minutes, he waved at my mom who turned and said, "Everybody out. We're gonna go look at this house." We all piled out and traipsed behind her up the sidewalk to the front door. She introduced us to the guy, whose name I can't remember, and we all went in.

It was a nice house, almost as big as our house at home, though it seemed funny 'cause it had almost no furniture in it. Mom led us through while Dad talked to the guy. When we finished the tour, we sat down on the steps. Dad asked, "Well, what do you think?"

"About what?" Tim wanted to know.

Dad looked at Mom and she shook her head "no". Dad continued, "We're buying this house and we're going to live here. What do you think?"

What do we think? What do we think? Cathy Rose started crying and the rest of us looked shell shocked. Then the questions flew like manure off the back of a spreader. "Why?" "What's wrong with our house?" "Do we have to move here?" "I hate this house. Can't we stay at our house?" And some choice comments. "I hate you." "This is not fair." "I'm not moving. I'll stay with my friend Charlie." The last one was from me.

There was a lot of pouting and crying and whining on the way home. Mostly there was confusion and fear. What was gonna happen? Why did this have to happen to us? We all went to bed sad, and though Mom tried hard to comfort each and every one of us, you could tell she was sad as well.

Later, they explained to us what had happened to force this move. If you remember, I told you Mom had two brothers, both of whom had left home early to move to the city and work there. Both got married, both had kids. Those were my cousins and we saw them several times a year. Apparently, my grandfather left the farm to his three children, equal shares, but with the proviso that my father would continue to be the farm manager and my uncles would get one third of the profits, if there were any, that the farm made. It was a family-owned dairy farm in the 80s. There were never any profits though I suspected my grandfather realized that and was kind of pimping his sons since they had up and left him.

But, and this is a big "but", Iowa farmland in the 80s was worth a fortune. My grandfather had assumed since the farm had been in the family for a gazillion years, no one would think of selling it. So he had not included a "must keep" provision in his will. It took the uncles (though Mom was sure it was actually the aunts) very little time to realize this oversight and demand the farm be sold. My parents could obviously not afford to buy out her brothers so the farm was listed and sold with crops in the fields and cows in the pasture. Oddly, the lawyers decreed all of the farm equipment belonged to my folks since it had all been purchased while Dad ran the farm.

With their third of the farm and all the crops and equipment, my parents had enough to buy a house in the city and keep bread on the family table 'til Dad found a job. Which proved to be a lot easier than they thought it would be. Midwest farmers, especially Iowa farmers, had a special relationship with the John Deere Company. During the depression, Deere was the one tractor company that reasoned that foreclosing on farmers and repossessing equipment helped no one. No one else would buy that equipment so the company let every farmer carry payments until they could afford to pay. It worked and with unintended consequences. Because they were the only company that kept farmers going, no self-respecting farmer would ever, and I mean ever, buy anything but a Deere ever again. It was a two way street. Deere took care of their farmers who took care of them. Within two weeks of leaving the farm, Dad became a regional dairy farm equipment rep for John Deere.

CHAPTER FOURTEEN

The day after we found out we had to leave the farm, I got up very early and pedaled over to Settler's. I sat on my bike at the edge of the woods until I saw old man Settler come bustin' out of the house, swearing like a madman, and gun his car out the lane. I coasted up to the porch and before I could knock on the door, Charlie came out.

"What's up?"

"We're moving to Davenport."

"Wh-wh-wh-what? Why?"

"Because my folks had to sell the farm. Stupid uncles wanted to sell it and we gotta leave."

"M-m-m-man that sucks."

"Tell me about it." That was the entire conversation. We went inside and Charlie's mom fixed us toast with her homemade jam for breakfast. We messed around in the barn for a while and then went down to our island where we spent the day flinging rocks and junk into the water and talking about all the fun we had had there. It made me very sad but I didn't let on.

A couple of days later, Charlie came over to our place while we were helping my dad sort out stuff in the barn which we were going to take with us. The pile wasn't very big on accounta we didn't need a lot of stuff for city life. Plus, mom said we had no place to put anything and to leave it all. Dad had decided to have a farm sale, but the farm buyers agreed to buy everything we left. As we shuffled our way through all the junk, Charlie pointed at a machine covered in about forty layers of dust and crap in the back of the loafing shed.

"What's that?"

"I dunno. Hey, Dad, what is that orange thing back there?"

Dad walked back to it and said, "It's a Gravely."

"What's that?"

"An old time walk-behind mower. Great for cutting brush. Hasn't been used since we got the bush hog for the tractor."

Charlie whispered to me, "Do you think your dad would sell it to me for cheap and let me pay him a little at a time?"

"I dunno. Hey, Dad, Charlie wants to know if he can buy it. He doesn't have the cash now, but he'd pay you for it."

Dad smiled and nodded his head, acting like he was thinking over the offer. Finally he walked over to Charlie and put his hand on Charlie's shoulder. "Yeah, I think I can let you have it, say, for one dollar?" Charlie just stared at him.

"Are you serious, Mr. Williams?"

"So we have a deal?" and Dad put his hand out to shake on it. Charlie pumped his hand. "I can deliver it for you but that's an extra quarter. I gotta tell you, though, I'm not sure it still works. It hasn't been run in probably ten, fifteen years." I fished a quarter out of my pocket and told Dad I'd pay for the delivery.

The day before we moved, Tim, Cathy Rose and I got invited by Mrs. Settler to come for lunch. We had toasted cheese sandwiches and potato chips and she had made us a going away cake which said "Good Luck" in icing. When Cathy Rose saw it, she started to cry and then Carol started crying. We hung out on the porch after lunch and later Mrs. Settler came out and told us our mom had called for us to come home and we said our goodbyes and then Charlie did the strangest thing. He hugged me. It was weird but I promised we would come back every weekend and talk on the phone and have them down to our new house and we'd still be friends forever.

Four days later, I started seventh grade at Saint Aloysius Junior/Senior High School. (Until I just typed that I had never thought about the fact that I went to school for six years at a place named for a saint who would have fit in now—he died as a result of caring for the victims of a serious epidemic.) We always just called it St. Al. I was scared to death. Besides being the new kid, we changed rooms for classes and had a bunch of different teachers. Plus, a home room teacher. Mine was Miss Mary Margaret Anderson. She was about a thousand years old and had gray hair and was chubby and short and wore really long dresses. Her hair was tied up on top of her head and her glasses sat on the end of her nose. She looked like she would be a pushover. She wasn't.

The very first day she assigned us seats and introduced herself and then read the daily announcements which everyone except me and a few dweebs ignored. Afterwards, she gave us a copy of the student handbook and told us, in her high squeaky voice, to read it and be quiet until the bell rang. Two guys in the back of the room immediately started joking around. Miss Anderson walked to the back of the room, grabbed the first kid, a dork named Kenny, by the ear and marched him up to the front of the class where she had him empty his back pockets and bend over and grab her desk. She produced this huge wooden paddle with holes in it (to reduce air cushion and increase the sting) and stood behind him for like ten minutes. When he finally started to whine, she hit him on the butt three or four times. He tried hard not to cry but he did. When she told him to return to his seat, he slunk back and slid into his seat, winching when he did. Miss Anderson asked, "Does anyone else want to talk ?" We all looked at our feet.

Anyway, sometimes in DeWitt I felt like a second-class citizen, like I said earlier. Here, I felt like I would have to move up six or seven classes to be second class. These kids all seemed so much older and way cool. I had gone from semi-cool to super nerd in one day. I kept my head down and my mouth closed, at least until third period which was math class taught by none other than my horror room teacher, Miss Anderson. I found a desk in the very back and couldn't believe it when Red Palmer walked into the room. We spied each other immediately and she made a beeline for me, sitting right behind me. We grabbed hands and she squeezed real hard. She started chattering so I turned around and held a finger to my lips to quiet her. I whispered I'd explain later. Turned out I didn't have to. Miss Anderson repeated her attention-getting performance with this class as well. This time with some cute girl named Heather who wouldn't shut up no matter how many people tried to shush her. Live and learn.

As soon as the bell rang, Lynne hugged me and thanked me. I asked her, "What are you doing here? Why aren't you at home?"

"My 'rents decided to move here to be closer to my dad's work and wouldn't let me stay with my older sister in DeWitt. It really sucks. I'm so glad you are here. I don't know anyone and the girls here aren't nice." She stopped talking and glared at me. "What are you looking at?"

I blushed and stammered, "Nuthin." But I'd been staring at the boobs she had sprouted since last spring. Luckily, before I could dig myself in deeper, the bell rang and I told Lynne I would see her later and trotted off to find my next class. Which was religion. I figured as much—me thinking about boobs and all and then having to think about Jesus and all.

Religion was taught by Father Dave Bouvier. I liked him immediately. There was just something about him. He didn't yell at kids to make them quiet down. He just stood quietly in the front and smiled and waited until we settled. He was tall and kinda looked like he'd be a good baseball player. He had dark hair that was gray around the edges and smiley eyes. After he had our attention, he introduced himself and talked a little about what we would be studying this year.

He asked us, "Where do you think you find Jesus?" Everyone either looked at their desks or their hands or their shoes.

Finally a girl in the back said, "Doesn't He live in that big cup thing in the church? Or somewhere in the church?"

Father Bouvier smiled and said "Well, not exactly." He paused. "Actually, you are right." The girl grinned broadly. "Christ is in that chalice. In fact, He's everywhere. In this room, in your books, in the grass outside, in the clouds and trees and your dog sleeping on the porch at home. He's in the food in your lunchbox, He's in clothes you have on, He's in the handbasket your grandmother puts flowers in."

Father continued talking about what he thought the nature of God and Jesus were, but I don't remember exactly what else he said. My mind had wandered off, like it seemed to do more and more. Christ in a handbasket. I liked that. I'd try to remember it.

I talked to a few kids in my classes and, probably because I was new, they were pretty nice. Nobody spit on me or anything and most everyone just ignored me which was fine. I saw Lynne once more that day. She was in my history class and we exchanged phone numbers. Our history teacher was this little guy, what we woulda called the runt of the litter. His name was Vernon Van der Derk, but the kids called him either der Dork or VD, both of which caused laughter. I had to ask my brother Chris why that was funny. That's when I learned about venereal disease. Gross.

Our final class of the day was Phys Ed, which was also taught by der Dork. The first day of Phys Ed turned out to be like every day of Phys Ed all year long. I hated it. The class lasted fifty minutes. The first ten, we did calisthenics, the next ten we ran laps and the last thirty we played artillery, which the rest of the world called dodgeball. But instead of those cushy red rubber balls, we used old volleyballs the high school teams had discarded because they were worn and misshapen. Which meant they hurt like hell when they hit you and they wouldn't fly straight.

Phys Ed is where I learned about the cruelty of junior high. There were 25 of us in the class, mostly scrawny or tubby twelve-year-olds, all going through the initial phase of adolescence. Old der Dork lined us up by height and had us count off. Odds on one side; evens on the other. Two guys were much bigger than the rest of us. Russell was just big. Quiet but big. Big, like a front end loader.

Scott Olsen was big because he was older. His folks had held him back a year and then he managed to flunk a year, so he was fourteen. He was not particularly tall, but he had broad shoulders and lots of muscles. I had never seen a guy walk like he did. Shoulders back, ramrod straight and he rolled his shoulders as he walked, as if he were strutting downhill. Wavy blond hair and a wispy blond mustache.

Der Dork chose one side to be on and rolled eight balls onto the court. Olsen grabbed the first one, wheeled and, from maybe three feet away, smashed the ball into a little kid's face, busting his glasses and bloodying his nose. I thought that would make der Dork stop the class. It didn't. I ran around like a madman dodging balls as best I could. In other words, I was out in less than a minute, hit in the back by der Dork himself. The only good thing that happened all class was when Russell nailed der Dork in the balls and made him grab his crotch and moan. Der Dork played no more that day. The entire rest of the year, we all tried, mostly in vain, to avoid Scott.

CHAPTER FIFTEEN

The first two weekends we lived in Davenport, my mom took us up to see Charlie and Jimmie. I think she used it as an excuse to go see some of her friends. It was great, being back on our own turf with the guys. Charlie had been working on his new mower and had actually gotten it started. He told me he had torn the thing entirely apart, mostly because he knew nothing about motors and wanted to see how it worked. When I told my dad about it, he was impressed Charlie had even gotten it back together, let alone gotten it working.

The second weekend he had it cutting brush. He told me he had spent about thirty hours working on it and that it was lots of fun. I asked him what he was going to do with it, like maybe sell it.

"H-h-h-h-heck, no. I'm going to cut people's grass and brush with it to make money," he grinned.

We rode our bikes over to our old place. The two guys who had bought the place—Mom called them "bachelor gentlemen farmers" were there, working on the house. I told them who we were and the older one was real nice and let us hang around. He told us they had hired a company to do the real farming, but that they were going to do the gardening and yard and stuff. Before we left, Charlie had worked out a deal to cut their grass in exchange for some pay and for being able to use the hay mow basketball court.

It was still sad leaving to go home, but by the third weekend, we had stuff going on and couldn't go to Settler's. Charlie and Jimmie and Carol came down around the first week of October for a sleepover and we showed them around town, making plans for them to come down to go trick or treating. When we went, I took Charlie with a couple of the new guys I had met, but he didn't seem to like that. He stuttered a lot and didn't say much. Later

I asked him if he didn't like the guys. All he said was, "They're okay, I guess."

At Christmas, we went up to make the rounds in DeWitt and drop off Christmas gifts, including a big basket to the Settlers. Charlie and I didn't have much to talk about. He was on the seventh grade basketball team and was a starter. I was on our team but was a bench warmer. He had really gotten into motors and spent lots of time studying them and finding old junk ones to work on. I hung around a lot with my new friends and told Charlie about them, but he didn't seem too interested. Like I wasn't interested in his motors.

In retrospect, it's really sad how we let friends slip away and don't make the minimum effort to stay current in their lives. After the first of the year, we didn't talk with or see each other again. He was still my best friend. But he was out of my life.

PART TWO

CHAPTER SIXTEEN

"Hey, Williams, wait up," Stone yelled down the hall for me. I stopped and waited for him to catch up.

"What up, Stone?"

"D'jasee Coach posted the notice for tryouts?"

"Duh. I was the first to sign up."

Stone was my main man. We had been buds since halfway through seventh grade when I got into a fight with Scott Olsen in a pick-up basketball game in Lindsay Park. I had thrown an elbow which caught Scott in the side of the head, a gesture he objected to by punching me in the nose. Stone, whose real name was Charles Robert Miller, jumped on Scott and wrestled him to the ground. Not that it helped that much—my nose was already broken—but I did appreciate the effort.

All three of us were on the seventh grade basketball team and bad blood had been brewing between me and Scott for a couple of months. Scott and Stone were starters, I was sixth man. In practices, I was always guarding Scott and a lot of shoving, body checking and elbow throwing went on. The fight seemed to clear the air. He and I were never gonna be pals, but when he saw the plastic nose guard I had to wear which made the guys laugh at me, he apologized and we were cool. By the end of the eighth grade basketball season, the three of us were the core of the basketball team. Stone and I underneath and Scott on point. And here it was, early in our freshman year and b-ball season was firing up already.

It's funny. I really don't remember a lot about junior high. Part of it is that we had moved to town at the beginning of seventh grade. Part was going from being a farm boy to a city guy. Part was having new friends. But mostly, I think it was making the jump from kid to teen. For one thing, at the end of sixth grade, I was four foot eight and at the beginning of ninth grade I was an even six feet tall. I had grown 16 inches in 27 months and, mostly, I just ate and slept. It seemed like I had to get a new pair of jeans every three months. My mom yelled at me constantly on accounta how much I was eating and my legs ached all the time. My feet flopped around whenever I ran and I couldn't be trusted not to drop glasses or plates or anything breakable.

My voice had squeaked for what seemed like years though it was probably only a couple of months. I started to shave, at least my upper lip. My pits were always wet and smelly. In fact, the whole ordeal of going through puberty would have been a total fucking disaster if old Stone hadn't stolen *Playboy* magazines from his dad for us to pour over. Oh, yeah, and I had learned how to effectively use swear words.

Also, on the upside was Erica Denner, Stone's cousin. Although she was the same age as Stone and me, she had actually beaten both Stone and me to puberty and by the time we started eighth grade, Erica had a huge set of boobs. Which she showed off any way and any time she could. I was one lucky guy. Erica decided I was going to be her boyfriend and, thus, became the first girl I ever kissed. We were still a couple a year later. I did like her. In addition to her obvious attributes, she was smart and funny and liked to just hang out and play video games and watch horror movies. I don't have to tell you the bonuses of watching horror movies with teen girls.

Stone was Stone when I met him, a nickname, like Cutter, which had no positive origin. But Stone was a much cooler name. Junior high is generally where the oddball names and nicknames we carry through life attach themselves to us. I was lucky, I guess, in that Cutter was deemed weird enough. Charles was renamed Stone by a comment from a nun, who asked him in third grade, when he couldn't answer a simple arithmetic question, "What is your brain, a stone?" All things considered, it could have been a lot worse. In our class alone, we had Tommy Peters who became Little Tommy Peters who became Little Peter which morphed into Dickie. Jack Horner became Jack in the Corner which because of the movie *Dirty Dancing* became Baby, as in "no one puts Baby in the corner." Nor were the girls immune. Erica became Erotica and Lynne, of course, was Red (after I spilled the beans). Harold Ball became Hairy Balls. Phil Buckle became Bill Fuckle. No one escaped.

I should point out that no one called Lynne, Red, more than once. Not because she would pound them like she did in grade school, but because she was dating Scott Olsen who offered anyone who called her Red, the opportunity to get punched. Except me. I was allowed to call her that when no one was around.

I walked with Stone down to the sign-up sheet. There were already about 20 guys signed up. "How many freshmen ya' think'll make the JV team?" Stone asked.

I thought about it a minute. "Not sure. Since it's only freshmen and sophomores, I'd guess five or six."

Stone grinned. "Yeah, that's what I figured. So you and me and Olsen gotta make it, right?"

"I hope so. The tenth graders have got a couple of big guys so Coach may be looking for some more guards. That one guy's gotta be like six four or six five. I'm sure you and Olsen'll make it. If I do, I'll probably be picking splinters out of my ass all year long. But, yeah, I think I'll make it." I was being modest. I knew I'd make it. Maybe not see a lot of playing time this year, but next year, I'd be a starter.

The following Monday evening tryouts started. There were 22 guys. We ran, shot baskets, played three on three and shot foul shots. After three days, three of the guys had taken themselves out. After practice on Friday, Coach made his first cut. Down to 15. Twelve would make the team. It would be close but I was gonna make it.

The next Monday evening Stone and I got to the gym just as the varsity practice was ending. When they left the floor headed for the locker room, one of the kids stayed at the far end shooting baskets. He had long hair that flew around when he moved and he kinda reminded me of an old time pro baller named Pistol Pete Maravich. This guy was maybe six two or three, had very fluid moves and a sweet shot. The shot reminded me of someone, though I couldn't put my finger on it.

We gathered around the coach at the east end of the court and he told us, "Okay, men, this is it. Last day to show me your stuff. I'll make the final cuts tonight. I want you all to know you have all done a great job and it's going to be difficult to see any of you go. You should all be proud of the effort you've made. I do wish I could keep more but twelve is the limit." He paused and looked down to the other end of the court. "Hey, Settler, hustle your butt down here."

I did a double take. What the hell? As Charlie trotted down the floor, I couldn't help but grin. He jogged to a stop right by me and said, "C-c-c-cutter, fa-fa-fa-fancy meeting you here," and chucked me on the shoulder. The other guys just stared at us.

The coach explained, "Gentlemen, this is Charlie Settler. Charlie is transferring into St. Aloysius next week and wants to play basketball for us. His folks asked if we could let him try out, so I had him work out with the varsity and we'll see how he does. Is that okay with you all?" There were some murmurs of dissent but only from the guys who were on the bubble. I thought it would be great.

We warmed up and the coach assigned us to teams and we played round robin games to ten buckets. I liked the fact the coach divided the teams fairly and especially that I was teamed with Charlie. It was just like the old days. About halfway through our second game, Olsen stole the ball from one of our guards and broke towards his basket. Charlie went in pursuit and as Scott went in for the easy lay-up, Charlie batted the ball away cleanly from behind. At that moment, I knew Charlie was in.

The next morning the list of the team went up. I wasn't on it. I was pissed. And embarrassed. Stone made it, as did Olsen and Charlie. I went home without talking to anyone. I must have slammed the door and stomped up to my room because five minutes later there was a light knock on my door. I ignored it.

"Cutter, are you okay?" My mom's voice was very soft.

"Yeah. Please leave me alone."

"Did something happen?"

I didn't respond and I heard my mom walk away. I pouted for a couple of hours, alternating between blaming everyone else and feeling sorry for myself. The coach was stupid and a bad coach. Olsen had somehow screwed me over. Charlie had stolen my spot. I was gonna quit high school. I hated everybody. Stupid assholes.

When no one came or called to tell me how badly I had been treated, I finally gave up and went downstairs to find something to eat. Though no one would care if I starved to death. My dad was sitting at the kitchen table.

"What happened, Winston?" Geez, he'd rolled out my real name. Now I must be in trouble.

"Nuthin."

"Well, if nothing happened, then lose the attitude."

"I didn't make the team."

My old man paused and then nodded his head. "Yeah, that sucks." My head jerked up. I had never heard my dad use that phrase. "Didn't do well at tryouts? Didn't hustle enough? Or just better players than you?"

"I thought I did okay." I looked at him and eventually heard what he was saying. Even though I didn't want to admit it, yeah, the guys who made the team were better than I was. I had done my best. It just wasn't going to be my game. I still had baseball and Stone's father had told us he would teach us golf in the spring. And if there was to be no basketball, I could try out for football next year. Everybody makes that team.

"Let's walk down to that new place, the 11th Street Precinct, and get some dinner. I understand they have a great tenderloin sandwich and a pool table." With that, he stood up and pulled on his jacket and yelled at Mom that we were leaving and would get something to eat out. I followed him out the door, already feeling better. I have lots of warm memories of my folks, and this one is right up there. A couple of hours later, I was full, jangling a bunch of quarters in my pocket, money I had won from him, and I was smiling. And until just this minute, I never realized he probably let me win.

On our way home, he said, "So I understand Charlie is coming to your school. I bet that makes you pretty happy, eh? Did his whole family move? Where are they living?" It kinda hit me like a brick to the side of the head. I'd been so tied up in the basketball thing, I hadn't even talked to him. When I got home, I tried calling him but their phone had been disconnected. I called a couple of the guys from my old school and nobody knew anything except Randy. He told me the family had all moved someplace and none of them were going to school in DeWitt.

CHAPTER SEVENTEEN

Charlie showed up the following week for classes. Since I was in college prep courses and he was in trade courses, our paths didn't cross. After class he had ball practice. I, of course, did not. The only time I saw him was a couple of times in the hall, hardly enough time to talk. I did ask him for his phone number, but he told me they didn't have one yet. I asked him where they were living and he mumbled something I couldn't understand.

A couple of weeks later I saw him talking with Lynne on their way to the gym after school. Lynne had made the junior varsity cheerleading squad. You could take the girl out of athletics, but you couldn't take the athletics out of the girl. Anyway, the next time I saw her, I asked if she could tell Charlie I would like to see him. She said, "Why don't you have him for dinner? I know he still eats. In fact, have us both. Like a reunion."

"Great idea. But won't Olsen get mad? You know, what with me being an old boyfriend and all."

Lynne laughed. "Yeah, I'm sure he's worried about my fifth grade boyfriend. Especially since it's you." She laughed again. I didn't think it was quite that funny.

That night I asked Mom if I could invite Charlie and Lynne over for dinner that Saturday. She said fine as long as they didn't mind spaghetti. I assured her they didn't. Lynne set it up with Charlie and they arrived together at six on the dot. The whole family ate and the chatter mostly was Charlie answering questions from my brother and sister about Jimmie and Carol. When I asked him about how he ended up at St. Al, he stuttered, "C-c-c-c-can we talk about i-i-i-it later?" Mom changed the subject to his basketball which didn't interest me.

After dinner, we went up to my room and both Lynne and I leaned on him for more info. He kinda drew into himself and darkened.

"Okay, g-g-g-g-guys, but th-th-this stays b-b-b-between us, okay?"

"Sure," we answered together. He told us his story. He stuttered a lot during the first part but then relaxed and by the time he was done, he didn't miss one beat.

"Remember when I broke my arm and it didn't get better and had to be rebroken?" We nodded and he continued, "I didn't fall off my bike. My dad broke it. He twisted it until it snapped because he didn't want me to waste time playing baseball. The doctors called the cops and the cops came to see us. Dad told us if we told, he'd beat us and then he'd beat Mom. So we lied. It wasn't the first time he hurt me. Sometimes he hit me, sometimes he hit my mom."

"What about the other kids?" Lynne asked.

"Mostly he just yelled at them. Sometimes he spanked them but usually just yelled."

"Why you and not them?" I asked.

His eyes closed, squeezed shut. When he opened them he looked first at me then at Lynne. "Because my dad isn't my dad." I heard air rush into lungs, though I don't know if it was Lynne or me.

"What the fuck?" I couldn't help my reaction. In my head was the phrase from the priest. Christ in a handbasket.

Lynne was a little better. "How do you know?"

"My mom told me."

"So you came here to live with your real dad?" Lynne asked.

"No. Mom doesn't know where he is." He looked away, then turned his face back to us. "Dad, I mean my old dad, got a job in Ottumwa so when they moved, Mom sent me here to live with an aunt. Actually she's not my real aunt, just my mom's oldest friend." He paused again and sniffled. "I really miss my family." He looked down so we were staring at the top of his head. Neither of us could think of anything to say. Finally, Lynne went over and sat next to him on my bed and put her arm around him.

We asked him if he knew anything about his real dad. Only his name. He was someone his mom had worked with who left the town without ever knowing he had a son. Mr. Settler knew nothing about the guy and Charlie was about six before he found out he wasn't his father. That's when the beatings started. Lynne wanted to know why his parents had stayed together.

"We had no place to go. No money. Mom didn't even own a car. The only jobs she ever had were being a waitress and working in a laundry at a hospital."

We talked about the old gang and the school. Charlie told me he had spent most of the summers cutting grass and weeds with the Gravely Dad gave him. The first summer alone he made over $700, but when his dad found out, he made Charlie give him half of it. Called it "room and board". The next summer, he didn't tell his parents about the money. He made over $1000. He was saving it to buy a car. His plan was to buy one and fix it up and learn how to repair motors at the same time.

We agreed to keep getting together for dinner as often as we could and I begrudgingly told them I would come to their basketball games. Charlie right out asked me if I blamed him for not being on the team.

"I gotta be honest. At first I did, but you were always better than me. And smarter than me. In fact, if I weren't so good looking, you'd be a three time winner." It was the first time we all laughed.

We talked until Lynne's mom called because she was worried. Dad drove them home.

The only two freshmen on the team who were starters were Charlie and Stone. Charlie was a truly talented ball player. Not my words. I heard the coach tell a reporter that. He said Charlie would be on the varsity team the next year. My thought, of course, was that maybe it would make a position available for me then. (It didn't.) As promised, I went to all the home games. By Christmas break they were unbeaten.

Shortly after the new year started, we had dinner at Ross' Restaurant over towards Bettendorf. Charlie lived on Hazelwood on the west side so he stopped by my house on his way and my mom drove us to the restaurant. When we got there, Lynne, who lived within a couple of blocks, was just walking up. She walked up to Charlie and hugged him, and before I could get upset she didn't hug me, the two of them started holding hands. At dinner Lynne told me she had broken up with Scott because, in her words, "He's a jerk." Duh.

A couple of weeks later, during one of their games, the refs called a time out when one of the opposing players twisted his ankle. Scott sidled up to Charlie and whispered to him, "So, Ch-ch-ch-ch-charlie, is Palmer putting out for you like she did for me? That's some g-g-g-g-good pussy, ain't it?" Charlie turned to walk away and Scott said loud enough for everyone to hear, "You know, she's fucked half the guys in our class." Charlie wheeled around and hit Scott so hard he went down like a sack of feed. His head bounced off the floor and he was out cold.

Stone flew off the bench and he and a ref kept Charlie from doing more damage. They cleared the floor, medics attended to Scott and Charlie was sent to the locker room. Scott was transported to the hospital where he was treated for a concussion and kept overnight for observation. By the end of the evening, Charlie was kicked off the team. Scott's parents wanted to have

Charlie arrested but school officials promised to deal with it harshly. Two days later, he was suspended from school for two weeks and then permanently barred from any interscholastic sports.

CHAPTER EIGHTEEN

Shawn Allen wore the same brown pants, or copies of the same brown pants, every day he came to school. The same brown shoes. The same dark shirt which may have been gray or blue or faded black. Most days he had a guitar strung across his back, forcing him to drag his backpack along his side. He was skinny with long brown hair which lay in tight curls on pale skin. The overall effect was a poorly dressed angel, down on his luck.

Shawn had moved to Davenport halfway through seventh grade, shortly after I had. He was quiet, not new-kid quiet but not-make-friends quiet. The guitar he carried was not for effect. He had been trained as a classical guitarist and had gotten permission from Mr. Davis, the music teacher/band director, to use the band room to practice. St. Al did not have an orchestra, middle school did not even have a band. It didn't seem to faze Shawn. Every day he would find a way to work in a period-long practice session. Davis claimed Shawn was a natural talent and would someday make it to the music big leagues. I wasn't sure what the music big leagues were but thought maybe that was like playing backup for Madonna.

Everyone liked him, but he didn't develop any close buddies until Charlie came to St. Al. Charlie had cut class one afternoon soon after he returned from his suspension and to avoid getting caught by a wandering assistant principal, ducked into the empty music room. While he was hiding behind the choir risers, Shawn came in and started playing. In fact, he immediately went into some fancy guitar thing though anything beyond the *ABC* song would be difficult as far as I was concerned.

Charlie wanted to leave but wasn't sure if Shawn would rat him out, so he stayed hidden. He couldn't believe one guy was making all those sounds on one guitar, so he popped his head up to see. Shawn saw him, smiled and raised one finger from a fret in salute. Charlie raised one finger in response and then stayed through the whole period listening. When the bell rang, he walked out of the band room and into the clutches of the assistant principal. He was about to be carted off when Shawn appeared and told the priest Charlie had been helping him and bluffed he had permission. Charlie couldn't believe this kid he didn't know had stood up for him.

As unlikely a pair as they were, they started hanging out together. Both were quiet and shy, but while Charlie was an athlete and was becoming somewhat of a gear head, Shawn was into the arts and reading and more cerebral pursuits. Like most kids in high school, they both sought out friends who would make them more complete. Shawn's dad worked downtown, so he started hanging out at Charlie's house after school, where his dad would pick him up on the way home.

Charlie had developed a little business of repairing lawn mowers and other garden equipment for his neighbors. He worked for a lot less than repair shops and it turned out he did a better job. Shawn was fascinated by how Charlie could use tools and his ability to make mechanical things work. He asked Charlie to show him how to work with tools and they hit upon an agreement. In exchange, Shawn would teach him how to play guitar.

"P-p-p-p-problem is," Charlie explained, "I don't have money to buy a guitar, so can you teach me on yours?"

"Actually, I have a couple of them. I'll bring you one over. That way, you can practice when I'm not around." Within just a few weeks, Charlie had learned the basics and they were doing duets of *Smoke on the Water*.

When school ended, Shawn asked if he could still come hang out at Charlie's.

"S-s-s-sure. If you want. I have some jobs cutting grass and I'm still fixing stuff, but whenever you want to hang out, come on over."

"Can I help with your work, you know, cutting grass and stuff? Maybe help with tool repairs?"

"I guess, but I can't pay you. I kinda need the money 'cause I have to buy my own food and crap. And I'm trying to save enough to buy a car to fix up."

"That's okay. I don't got anything else to do this summer."

The second week of summer, someone brought Charlie an old trailer to repair. It needed new wheel bearings and the guy brought the repair parts. Shawn helped him get it up on blocks and Charlie attacked the odd-shaped lug nuts with a pipe wrench. When he couldn't loosen them, he used a piece of pipe to increase the leverage and finally broke the lug nuts loose. Shawn watched the whole process.

Finally, Shawn said, "You'd think there would be an easier way to do that."

Charlie laughed. "Yeah, there's a lot easier way to do that. If you have the right tool." He laughed again.

"What tool is that?"

"It's called an impact wrench. Actually, with nuts this corroded, you should have a pneumatic impact wrench."

"What's that?"

"It's a wrench that kinda hammers the nut loose. It's powered by compressed air not electricity. So in addition to the tool itself you need an air compressor and the hoses." Shawn just nodded his understanding.

A few days later, when Shawn's dad dropped him off, he opened the trunk of his car and he and Shawn lifted out several boxes. Shawn carried the two smaller ones back to the garage. Charlie intercepted him on his way back to get the larger box. "Hey, Settler, can you help me carry that?" pointing at the large box by the driveway.

"W-w-w-what is it?"

"It's kinda a present for letting me hang out all the time and feeding me lunch and stuff." Charlie eyed him suspiciously, then opened the boxes containing an impact wrench, hoses and an air compressor. "I thought these might help if you have to do more stuff like the trailer."

"Wow. How did you get this stuff? This costs lots. I can't pay you for this stuff."

"Not asking you to. I figure maybe I can be sort of your junior partner, maybe, huh?"

"Heck, if you buy this kinda stuff, you can be the boss." Charlie grinned.

Towards the end of summer, Shawn asked Charlie, "Hey, you wanna come to dinner at my house?"

Charlie thought about his regular diet of Jeno's Pizza Rolls and Hot Pockets and it took him about half a second to say, "Hell, yes."

"Great. How about Friday I hang out during the day here and then Dad will pick us up after work. You wanna just spend the night? I got video games and stuff to play."

"Sure. Let me check with my aunt but I'm sure it'll be okay."

Friday, the guys spent the afternoon reassembling a lawn mower motor Charlie had for repair. As they finished up, Shawn said, "We probably oughta get cleaned up. Dad will be here in a few minutes." Charlie scrubbed his hands and face and put on a clean shirt. As he buttoned it up, he noticed, for the first time, that his hands, even when scrubbed clean, had, deep down in the pores and crevices, the grease that marked him as a mechanic. He smiled, thinking how it was a badge of honor not unlike how Shawn was proud of the guitar calluses on his fingertips.

When they arrived at Shawn's house, Charlie was shocked. The house was out in the country, off Kimberly Road, hidden from the road by ten acres of woods. Charlie had assumed, like everyone else, based on Shawn's dress and demeanor, his home would be modest, if not downright shack-like. It wasn't. It was huge. Shawn's dad was a lawyer at a firm which handled mostly real estate. His dad realized the real money was on the other side of the table. He had the right moxie at the right time in the right place and made a fortune in real estate development.

Charlie more or less cowered in the corner of the backseat, taking it all in. There was a large brick house, bigger even than the farmhouse I had lived in, there was a four car garage and a swimming pool behind the house. He felt way out of place.

"C'mon," Shawn said, jumping out of the car as it rolled to a stop. "Let's go up to my room," and he bounded up the massive front steps to the huge front door. Charlie could not respond but fell in right behind Shawn because he didn't want to be alone here. Charlie took it all in, from the formal living room with expensive rugs to the fancy chandelier in the dining room. As he started up the steps, Shawn yelled toward the back of the house, "Hey, Mom, call us when dinner is ready. We're starved."

Charlie stayed right on his heels. Shawn's room was huge with its own personal bathroom and a TV and music system and about a gazillion guitars. "Wh-wh-wh-why didn't you tell me you're rich?"

"Aw, we're not rich. Dad does pretty well at his job and the one thing my mom wanted was a big house, so Dad built this for her." He paused. "Mom was pretty poor growing up so Dad thought she should get what she wanted." They checked out all of Shawn's stuff and played around with the guitars until his mom yelled to come to dinner.

Charlie froze at the entry to the dining room. The table was set with all kinds of glasses and silverware and plates and candles and serving dishes. Mrs. Allen had on a dress and Mr. Allen still had on his suit. Charlie grabbed Shawn by the sleeve and Shawn read the fear in Charlie's eyes. Shawn whispered, "C'mon. It's just dinner." Charlie didn't move. Shawn looked at his parents and shrugged.

Shawn's dad stood up and took off his suit coat and tie, rolled up his sleeves and said, "Let's go, guys. Food's getting cold." Charlie followed Shawn to the table and sat next to him, staring at all the place settings.

Shawn whispered, "Just do what I do. You'll like this. It's Quiche Lorraine."

Charlie did as told and took a bite. His eyes lit up and he said, louder than he meant to, "Hey, th-th-th-this is really good."

Shawn's mom said, "Thank you," and his dad hid a smile. By the end of the evening, Charlie had relaxed and was completely infatuated with the entire Allen family.

CHAPTER NINETEEN

We finally got to the best year of high school, tenth grade. Sophomores. No longer the dinks of school. The year we could get our driver's licenses and get some well-deserved freedom. It was gonna be the finest year yet. Real dates. Hanging with the guys. Most of us had had summer jobs and had a little money in our pockets. Sure, we weren't as cool as the seniors, but they'd be gone soon.

Over the summer, I'd seen Lynne lots since she lived in the neighborhood where I cut grass and did odd jobs. She told me things had cooled between her and Charlie, that they just hadn't seen much of each other. I asked her how he was and she said "Okay," and nothing else. She had introduced me to a girl in her neighborhood who went to Bettendorf High named Nancy Legget. Nancy was on the swim team and was about the coolest girl I ever met. Lynne told me I should ask her out and even though I knew I'd get shot down, I did. By the end of summer, we were kind of a thing. You understand, cheeseburgers and movies and holding hands. I wasn't what you might call precocious when it came to, well, you know.

As always, the first few days of the school year were spent renewing friendships, figuring out the teachers and checking out the new kids. I saw Charlie and we caught up on the summer. He'd bought a car, a 1980 Datsun 280Z. I don't have to tell you that even though it was ten years old, that was one hot car. He'd gotten it cheap since it needed a lot of work, but he was gonna do that himself. We talked about cutting grass, I told him about Nan (to which he said, "Nan and Win. C-c-c-c-ute," and laughed) and he told me about Shawn and learning guitar and about breaking up with Lynne. We ran out of things to say. Which was sad.

We did have one class together. Music. Though it really wasn't music. It was learn-to-sing-hymns class. The nun taught us absolutely nothing about music just about how to sing church songs like good Catholics. Christ in a handbasket. There were four new kids in our grade, two of them in the music class, Alan Johnson and Regan Renarde. Everyone noticed when Alan walked into class the first day. The guy was like six eight, all arms and legs. He couldn't have weighed 175 pounds soaking wet and looked like he'd have to be staked down not to blow away in the wind. Stone, who was standing next to me on the riser, whispered, "Geez, Cutter, if that guy can walk and chew gum at the same time, I think he just took your spot on the b-ball team." Turned out he could not sing a note, but he was a pretty fair baller.

Alan climbed to the top of the riser which made him seem even taller. Charlie walked in a minute later and ended up standing next to Alan. They talked and I saw them fist bump, so they must have already discovered something in common. Alan would have kept most folks' attention throughout class had it not been for the other newbie.

Regan was the first honest-to-god goth St. Al had ever seen. We didn't even know the word "goth". She was maybe five six and slender with beautiful eyes and hair dyed so black it was almost blue. Her skin was very white even by Midwest standards. Ghostly. Black lipstick, black eyeliner and some kind of small jewel stuck to the side of her nose which turned out to be a piercing, something that gave me the willies.

Stone whistled very low. I rolled my eyes at him. He whispered, "I think I'm in love. Or at least lust." Regan walked over to the girls' side of the risers and climbed to the end of the top tier, her head down and her long hair falling in front of her face.

Sister Delia walked in and the room quieted. She introduced herself, then asked everyone to introduce themselves, starting in the back with the girls.

Which meant Regan had chosen the worst spot possible. She didn't lift her head and kinda mumbled her name.

"I'm sorry, Miss. We can't hear you. Please take the hair out of your face and speak up."

Regan tucked the hair behind her ears and said only slightly louder, "Regan Renarde, Sister."

Sister Delia continued around the room. When she got to Alan, she said, "My, you're a tall one, aren't you?" No duh, I thought. Except, apparently, I didn't just think it. Sister wheeled toward me and asked, "Do you have something to add, Mr. Williams?" Stone started laughing. "And you, Mr. Miller? Why don't you two gentlemen join me down here." It wasn't a question. I could feel my face flush. We shuffled down next to her.

After the introductions were done, she had us pass out hymnals. Stone was quick to go to the girls' side and walked directly back to Regan. He gave her his best smile and hello. She took the hymnals and did not acknowledge him. When we returned to our place on the risers, I whispered, "He drives. He shoots. Aiiiir…..balllll…"

"Please turn to Hymn Number 24, *Faithful Cross*." She pushed a couple of buttons on the ancient sound system and scratchy music came out of the two wall speakers behind us. She raised her hand and, on cue, we started singing. It was pretty obvious our hearts were not in it. We finished the first verse and she turned off the music. "Okay, that wasn't as bad as I expected," she said, "but it was very bad. On the second verse, I want just the men to sing." It sounded substantially worse than the first verse. In fact, she stopped us halfway through.

"Ladies, why don't you show them how to sing it?" She started the music and the girls sang louder than they had before. Nothing like a little gender competition to fire things up. Then an odd thing happened. The girls, first the ones near the back, then slowly the rest of them, stopped singing and turned their faces to the end of the back row. Regan had her eyes closed and continued to sing, unaware she was singing alone. To a person, we could not believe what we were hearing. Her voice was incredible, high and clear and, well, amazing. By the time we were all silent, she finally opened her eyes and stopped midnote. "What?" she demanded.

Sister Delia smiled. "I think, Miss... I'm sorry, what is your name again?"

"Regan Renarde."

"Well, I think, Miss Renarde, your singing has done something no one in this school has ever done. You got sophomores to be silent. You have a beautiful voice and I am so happy to have you join us." Regan's pale, white complexion turned pink and she looked at her feet. I noticed as we returned to singing, the girls around Regan sang very quietly.

In the cafeteria during lunch, Charlie was telling Shawn about Regan and her voice when she came in, bought her lunch and found a place to sit. By herself. She sat, head down, trying to avoid the looks and gestures aimed in her direction. Shawn stood up and said, "Let's go talk to her." Before Charlie could answer, Shawn was on his feet, threading his way back to her table.

"Hi. You're Regan, right? I'm Shawn." He stuck a thumb in Charlie's direction who was slowly making his way to the table. "My friend Charlie told me about you in music class. He says you got a great voice."

Charlie sidled up to Shawn and nodded his head in greeting, "H-h-h-hey."

"Can we sit with you?" Shawn asked as he slid into a chair. Charlie remained standing. Regan said nothing and Shawn stuck out his hand towards her. "Nice to meet cha." Regan looked at his hand as if a dead fish was being waved in her direction. He left his hand hanging in the air and smiled. She finally took his hand and shook it once.

She looked up at Charlie, said, "Hey," and offered her hand to him. Charlie shook it and remained standing until she pointed at another chair. Charlie sat.

Shawn went on, "Charlie told me about your singing and I was wondering if you took lessons or something. I play a couple of instruments but can't sing worth crap."

She looked at Charlie. "Do you play an instrument too?"

"Sh-sh-sh-sh-sh..." Charlie stopped and took a couple of deep breaths. "Sh-shawn taught me how to play guitar. A little. B-b-but he's really good."

"You don't have to be nervous."

"I-I-I-I'm not. Sometimes I just stammer a little."

"I used to stutter a lot. In fact, my folks got me singing lessons to help me get better." She stopped and blushed slightly. "I mean, not to get better, but just so I wouldn't stutter so much." She smiled at Charlie. They stared at each other and Charlie smiled back.

"Hey," Shawn said, trying to get their attention. "I really like your outfit. We don't see much like it around here. What's the chain for?" He pointed to the chain which looped from her waist down to her knee. Her jeans were black denim with silver studs down the outside seam and there were holes in the knees. She also wore a lightweight black turtleneck even though the temperature was almost 90.

"It's a wallet chain," she explained, pulling a black studded wallet out of her hip pocket. "Mostly it's just there for looks. I don't even have anything in the wallet." She laughed a little.

"C-c-c-cool," Charlie said.

Shawn nodded. "So if you wanna hang out sometime or something, Charlie and I mess around with guitars out at my house. I mean, when Charlie doesn't have his head buried under the hood of his car." He took out a piece of paper and wrote his number on it and slid it across the table.

Regan took the number and slid out of her chair. "See ya." And she was gone.

CHAPTER TWENTY

The first week of school, the football coach had tryouts for the underclassmen. I figured since my chances of getting the highly coveted varsity letter in basketball had receded into oblivion, I should try out. As I said, everyone makes the football team. Our school record over the last ten years was like two and 80. I think the two were forfeits. Still, a guy could get a letter and it wasn't nearly as much running as basketball. And, yeah, they did give letters for baseball but that would impress like zero girls.

It took maybe half a dozen practices to discover the ugly truth. We only made the team to give the real players cannon fodder to pound into full body bruises. My six foot frame weighed in at a hefty 155, a bit too little to play line and because I was a bit too wussy to play defense, they put me at tight end. Which I thought was pretty cool since I could catch passes and score touchdowns and be the hero who won the game and all the girls would want to date me and the guys would want to be me.

Turns out catching a baseball does not translate into catching a football, nor does the padding a football player wears offer the same protection as my catcher's gear. The first time my number was called in practice for a pass across the middle, I hauled it in and picked up ten yards. First down. Sweet. The second time, same play, a senior linebacker who bore an uncanny physical resemblance to Arnold Swarzenegger lay in wait and hit me in the armpit as I stretched out for the pass.

The resultant broken ribs meant I got to sit on the bench the rest of the year. No letter. No playing time. On the upside, I got to be in the team photo and was the backup holder for the place kicker. The crap a guy will go through for female attention.

Stone had wanted to play but when the basketball coach got wind of Stone's trying out, he stormed into the football coach's office and you could hear the screaming match all the way to the gym. Seems you don't take a guy who would be starting varsity his sophomore year and turn him into bear bait. The principal agreed…I think because we were gonna compete for the league championship in basketball but were probably gonna be zero and whatever in football. Again. Someone who witnessed the Great Coach Title Bout said that the basketball coach, in an effort to quell the disturbance, did offer "I'll give you Scott Olsen. He's already cost me the best basketball player this school has seen in thirty years and I can do without his trouble making ways."

When Shawn told Charlie about the conversation, Charlie just spit on the ground and told him, "Hand me that wrench, wouldja?"

The fall passed pretty quickly. School, football practice, Friday night games, hanging out at each other's houses, Sunday morning mass, repeat. The really fun stuff of earlier years, like Halloween, didn't cut it anymore. We were too old to go trick or treating and too afraid to go vandalizing. Nancy had a Halloween party, and since we were still dating, I was anointed as a co-host. All the guys said it was a crappy party and while I had to defend Nancy, they were right. Her mom had to okay all of the activities, which meant instead of dancing and watching a horror movie and necking, we were stuck bobbing for apples and posing for pictures of our costumes.

But I didn't break up with Nancy, lame as her party was. The next weekend was Homecoming and the big time Homecoming dance. Only sophomores and older were allowed to go so it was kind of a big deal. And since Nancy didn't go to St Al, the only way she would get to go was if she was invited by a sophomore, namely, me. Breaking up with her would have resulted in her being pissed enough to remove me from my testicles, and I had actually grown quite fond of them.

The event was, like so many anticipated high school events, a total let down. Getting duded up was cool, buying the corsage felt all grown up and Nancy dressed up and her hair all done made me glad we dated. She was a knockout. But then we mostly just sat around at tables drinking Hawaiian Punch laced with 7-Up and watched some of the older kids dance. I made a mental note to cross school dances off the list.

The high point of the evening, other than seeing all the guys ogling Nancy, was when Shawn Allen and his date, the goth girl, walked in. Everybody was in suits or even tuxes and the girls were all dressed to the nines (actually, I didn't and don't know what that means, but I heard my mom say it once) and we thought we were pretty damned cool...until Shawn got there. Shawn was wearing his usual brown pants and what appeared to be a new black shirt, but he looked pretty much the same as he did every other day. Regan, however, had on a tight dress, floor length, but with a slit which went up practically all the way to her waist. The bottom and the ends of the extra-long sleeves were made to look like they had been shredded.

Her black make up was even more pronounced than what she normally wore. She looked like a classy version of Elvira. But without the campiness. She never lifted her eyes from the ground. They arrived pretty much after everyone had already seated themselves at the tables around the dance floor. That sounds way swankier than it was. The folding tables were borrowed from the cafeteria and were decorated with crepe paper bunting and paper flowers. They made their way slowly across the dance floor to find a seat at the far end of the gymnasium.

The reactions were priceless. After my initial "wow" reflex, I looked around the room. The guys, all of them, were staring with abject envy; their dates, with the slitted eyes of jealousy; and the parent/teacher chaperones with the panic of helplessness. I laughed out loud.

"What?" Nancy demanded.

"Look at everyone's expressions," I said, waving my arm around the room. "It feels like I'm watching some movie where I'm the only one who gets the joke." She looked around the room, looked back at Shawn and Regan and then started laughing as well. Stone and his date, who were sitting with us, didn't get it. I jumped up and grabbed Nancy's hand and said, "C'mon," and we headed across the floor to Shawn's table. When we got there, I was shocked to see Charlie sitting with them. He was impeccably dressed in black jeans, black shoes and a long sleeved black shirt with a mandarin collar buttoned all the way to the top. He appeared to be dateless.

My immediate reaction was "cool" until I noticed Nancy staring at him, unconsciously wetting her lips with her tongue. Not that he noticed. He was too busy staring at Regan. They looked like they belonged together. He finally looked up and saw me, took a second to recognize me and then smiled. He rose quickly and stuck out his hand.

"C-c-c-cutter!" It had been a couple of months since we last spoke and it was good to hear his voice. He had dropped the music class, so we only saw each other occasionally across our small campus. Our classes and activities just didn't bring us into contact.

"Nice threads. You taking a class in fashion or sump'en?"

"F-f-funny." He turned to Nancy and said, "Th-th-this must be the famous Nan we have heard so much about," and reached to shake her hand. She blushed and remained speechless but let him hold her hand.

"Well, old home week, eh?" Shawn said. He introduced himself and Regan to Nancy and then said, "Why don't you guys join us? We're here mostly because we wanted to hear the band, but also because Regan has never been to a dance before." I looked at her and found that exceedingly hard to believe.

"Thanks, but we should really get back to Stone and his date. You know Stone, if we didn't sit with him, he'd be alone all night." Charlie laughed. "Just wanted to say 'hi' and act like we belonged with you cool kids." I looked at Charlie and added, "Let's grab a burger sometime. If you can work me into your schedule."

He nodded and grinned and said, "Sure."

Turned out the reason they were so interested in hearing the band was they had put together their own band and had been booked to play at the Christmas dance. Though we didn't learn that until the night of that dance.

CHAPTER TWENTY-ONE

Charlie was bent over the front fender of the 280Z, half of his body in the engine compartment, changing the timing chain when Shawn told him about the coaches' fight. He acted like he was ignoring the comment the coach made about him being the best basketball player in the last thirty years, but he smiled into the greasy engine. "Hand me that wrench, wouldja?"

Shawn passed him the wrench and said, "You know your problem, Settler? You spend all your friggin' time studying or with your head buried in that car."

"Your point?" came the muffled reply.

"Well, frankly, you're no fun."

Charlie kept his head buried, tightened down the last bolt and smiled. He was getting closer. He'd cleaned out the cylinders, replaced the pistons and replaced the cylinder head. He could almost hear the roar of the engine and feel the power from the motor. He rose to his full height and stretched his back. "What'dya mean, I'm no fun? I'll remind you of that when we're tooling around in this beast... Unless of course your daddy buys you a Beamer and you are too high class to ride in my car."

Shawn flinched a little even though he knew Charlie was kidding. It always made him uneasy when someone referred to his family's money. "Yeah, you're probably right. But I can't decide between the Beamer and a Porsche. Which one do you think Regan would like better?"

It was Charlie's turn to flinch though Shawn wouldn't pick up on it. "I'm pretty sure she'd rather walk than ride around in any fancy schmancy car. Now one that a guy had personally restored? That, she'd be interested in."

Shawn stared at his friend for a minute, then went on, "Speaking of your being boring as hell these days, Regan's coming over to my house Friday and we're gonna play around with some music. You wanna come? Have some pizza, play some tunes. You can stay the night. What'dya think?"

Charlie squinted one eye in Shawn's direction. "Sure. I'm in."

Shawn's dad picked them up at Charlie's house late Friday afternoon and, when they got to Shawn's, a huge Ram dually, roaring loudly and belching smoke, pulled in behind them. The guy behind the wheel was a freckle-faced kid in his twenties who looked like he was thirteen. He was wearing a snap-button western shirt and a cowboy hat. He practically skidded to a halt which, had the driveway not been paved, would have stirred up a huge cloud of dust. He rolled down his window, touched the brim of his hat and said, "Howdy."

Regan jumped out of the passenger side, kept her eyes down and sidled over to Shawn. The kid ground the gears putting the truck in reverse, turned around and waved his hat out the window. Shawn and Charlie looked at each other, then they looked at Regan who was still staring at the ground. Finally, Mr. Allen said, "What the hell was that?"

Shawn and Charlie both laughed. Regan's pale complexion turned bright red. In a tiny voice she told him, "I'm sorry, Mr. Allen. That's my brother Joey. When we moved from Philadelphia, he thought he was moving to the Wild West and decided to be a cowboy."

Shawn's dad smiled and then started laughing. "Yeah, cowboying is a big thing here in the Quad Cities," and laughed again.

They exchanged the obligatory niceties with the parents, grabbed some chips and Cokes and made their way to Shawn's room. They messed around until the pizza arrived, ate in the dining room and went back to playing with the music. After they'd played several songs, mostly simple so Charlie could play along, Regan asked, "Do you know how to play *Don't Think Twice, It's All Right* by Bob Dylan? I know it's kinda old, but it's one of my favorites."

"I've got a Dylan songbook here someplace," Shawn told her and started digging around in his piles of music. Two minutes later he pulled it out and blew the dust off it. "Got it." He thumbed through the pages and stopped, looked at the music and blew out a low whistle. "Wow, this is kinda tough. Four chords. But I'll give it a go." He placed the music on the keyboard stand and stood behind her. After a couple of minutes of experimenting with the cords, he said, "Okay. Let's try it."

He did the intro and they started playing. And then she started singing,

"It ain't no use to sit and wonder why, babe
It don't matter, anyhow
An' it ain't no use to sit and wonder why, babe
If you don't know by now
When our rooster crows at the break of dawn
Look out your window and I'll be gone
You're the reason I'm trav'lin' on
Don't think twice, it's all right
It ain't no use in turnin' on your light, babe
That light I never knowed
An' it ain't no use in turnin' on your light, babe
I'm on the dark side of the road
Still I wish there was somethin' you would do or say
To try and make me change my mind and stay
We never did too much talkin' anyway
So don't think twice, it's all right
It ain't no use in callin' out my name, boy
Like you never did before
It ain't no use in callin' out my name, boy
I can't hear you anymore
I'm a-thinkin' and a-wond'rin' all the way down the road
I once loved a young man, a child I'm told
I give him my heart but he wanted my soul
But don't think twice, it's all right
I'm walkin' down that long, lonesome road, babe
Where I'm bound, I can't tell
But goodbye's too good a word, boy
So I'll just say fare thee well

I ain't sayin' you treated me unkind
You could have done better but I don't mind
You just kinda wasted my precious time
But don't think twice, it's all right..."

Charlie stared at Regan. As usual, she sang with her eyes closed. As she finished, they were both pulled from their reveries by the sound of softly clapping hands outside the door. Shawn used his guitar to point first at Charlie and then at the door. Charlie opened it and Mr. and Mrs. Allen stood in the hall applauding. Before Shawn could protest their listening in, his mom said, "That was amazing. You guys sound terrific." Regan blushed. "I especially like how you made Dylan's song into a female anthem. Just wonderful."

Regan stared at the floor. Mr. Allen told them, "You should put together a band. You are really good." He apologized for interrupting and they went back downstairs.

Shawn said, "Sorry 'bout that. They're always butting in."

"That's okay," from Regan. "I think it's kind of neat they're interested in what you do."

They turned quiet, Charlie strumming his guitar, Regan humming some obscure tune. Finally, Shawn asked, "What do you think? Should we put together a little group to play some music? You know, you and me on guitar," nodding at Charlie, "her on keyboard and vocals and maybe find a drummer."

"I think I'm not good enough for that."

Shawn laughed. "Yeah, we know. Your job would be to play backup cords and look pretty. Though we might have to work on your wardrobe."

"Who'd we get as drummer?"

"I don't know. How about Scott Olsen?"

"F-f-f-fuck you."

Shawn and Regan laughed. "I take it you don't like him," she said.

"You're right."

Shawn told them, "There's a freshman named Beckett something-or-other who plays in drumline."

"He any good?"

"He's a she actually. And she is." He paused and grinned. He pointed at Charlie. "Did I mention she's really hot? You know, for a freshman." He quit grinning when Regan gave him a dirty look. "So, a plan?" They nodded.

CHAPTER TWENTY-TWO

"You okay?" Regan asked Charlie.

"Yeah. Why?"

"I dunno. You seem a little down or something."

"Nah. I'm fine. Maybe just nervous about this whole band thing." He paused, "You know, I kinda try to keep my head down 'cause of the whole problem I had with Olsen."

They were in the make-shift studio they'd put together in one of the Allen's four garages. Though make-shift sounds like it would barely do. In fact, it had pretty much everything you would need to record CDs. Charlie had been working on the cords for Phil Collins' *Another Day in Paradise*. Shawn was at the other end of the studio working with Beckett, whose last name was not "something-or-other" but Callaham. Shawn had been right. She was a very talented percussionist.

"C-c-c-can I ask you a question, Regan?"

"Sure."

"Why do you dress like that, you know, with the black clothes, the black hair, black lipstick and the pale skin?"

She smiled and thought for a minute. Then, "It actually has a name. It's called 'goth', though I'm not sure why. I got into it to hide, I guess."

"Hide? From what?"

"Myself. Who I was. You know I told you how I used to stutter and my folks got me into music to help with that. I always felt different from everyone. Kids would laugh at me when I would try to talk, so I just quit talking. I lived in my head, and that's not always a good place to take up residence, you know what I mean."

"Yeah I do."

"In seventh grade I got enrolled in this advanced music class and there were all these kids who were into these weird music groups, like Siouxsie and the Banshees and The Cure. Turned out they all kinda felt out of place and the music voiced their feelings, made them feel not so alone. I found it spoke to me the same way and helped me feel like I could fit in somewhere. You know? Funny, in order to fit in I had to dress weird and stay out of the sun and wear black makeup and we all ended up looking alike. Be just the same to be different. And the worst thing about it? I used to love going out in the sunshine, being at the pool, playing with my girlfriend."

Before he could stop himself, Charlie stood up, laid down his guitar and hugged her. He stood that way for a minute, feeling really happy until Shawn yelled over at them, "Hey, you fraternizing with the help, or somepin?" Charlie knew he was kidding but he pulled back. As he did, Regan put her hand on his arm and squeezed very hard.

The group decided if they were to be a real band, they needed a couple of things: a name and a setlist. And a leader. Shawn appointed himself leader. The others looked around at the Shawn-provided studio, equipment and instruments, shrugged their shoulders and happily agreed. Shawn had also picked out the name.

"We'll call ourselves 'Blake's Tyger'."

"Who's Blake?" Beckett asked and Charlie was glad that he wouldn't have to look stupid by not knowing.

"An old time poet. He wrote this great poem, *Tyger*," Regan said before Shawn could answer. "You know, as in 'Tyger Tyger, burning bright, In the forest of the night; What immortal hand or eye, Could frame thy fearful symmetry?'" They all stared at her and she blushed. "I liked it so I memorized part of it." She paused. "I think it's a great name."

"I don't get it," Beckett said.

"Y-y-you will," Charlie told her, "You will."

They each got to pick out four songs for the set and decided to practice at least twice a week. Charlie asked, "So, are we gonna do something, like, I don't know, try out for the talent show or something."

"Well," Shawn answered, "actually, I've talked to Mr. Davis, the band director, and he says after we get ready, he'll listen to us and see if maybe he can get us a gig somewhere, you know, playing for free or something."

A couple of weeks later after they finished practicing and Mr. Allen was driving everyone home, Charlie said to Regan, "Hey, my car is ready for a test drive. I still got a lot of work to do on the interior and it needs a paint job, but I'm gonna take it out for a test drive. You wanna go?"

Regan raised her eyebrows. "You have a driver's license?"

"A learner's permit."

"How could I go? Doesn't your car have just two seats? I don't have a license."

"W-w-w-we'll cheat a little," Charlie told her and winked.

"Okay."

Regan's brother once again dropped her off and ten minutes later Charlie eased the Z car out of the driveway and cautiously drove up to Telegraph Road, then up to Locust which he took west under I-280 and into the country. They'd driven a couple of miles when Charlie pulled the car into a dirt lane, took out a notepad and made a couple of entries.

"What are you writing?"

"The engine doesn't sound quite right. I just made a note of a few things to check."

"How do you know so much about cars?" Regan asked.

"I don't. Just stuff I've taught myself. I'm taking auto mechanics in school, but so far I've learned nothing I didn't already know."

"Did your dad teach you this stuff?"

"Hardly." He paused. "M-m-m-my stepdad didn't like me. He didn't teach us anything. I never knew my real dad."

"You didn't? Why?" But before Charlie could respond, she added, "I'm sorry. I'm prying."

"That's all right. It's okay," and Charlie told her about his mother and father and stepfather and his siblings. The whole story. She remained silent. After he finished, he stared out the front window. She got out of the car, walked to his side and opened the door and offered her hand. He took it and she pulled him out of the bucket seat. Then she hugged him. They stood like that for a couple of minutes and then she walked back around the car and got in.

"We'd better get back," she told him. "My brother's picking me up in about 20 minutes." They drove back in silence.

As they turned down his street, he said, "Hey, would you want to go to the Homecoming Dance with me?"

She didn't respond immediately. He looked over at her and she was staring at him. "I would love to but I already have a date. I'm going with Shawn."

"Okay," was all he said, though he felt a jolt of disappointment go through his shoulders.

CHAPTER TWENTY-THREE

Football season ended, thank the lord, and basketball season began, which meant that I was sportless. Stone had moved up to varsity and spent all his waking hours playing, practicing or thinking about b-ball. Or about his girlfriend. So I had squat to do. I called Charlie to see about grabbing a burger sometime. We set up a date, but then he couldn't make it. His mom had come to town and he wanted to spend some time with her. I spent more than enough time with my mom. In fact, by the end of Thanksgiving break, she suggested I move out. I didn't take her suggestion.

I was still dating Nancy, though I could sense her interest was waning. I figured she wouldn't break up with me until after Christmas. You know, so she could go to the Christmas dance and get a Christmas present. I asked my brother Jim, who was home from college for Thanksgiving, if I should break up with her first. He said, "Nah. Just buy her a cheap present." Count on Jim to teach me the asshole way of doing something. I did take his suggestion.

December turned really cold and it seemed we were cooped up in the house all the time. Of course, all the older kids in the family were gone so we weren't so packed in that we were ready to kill each other. John, who had gotten married the summer before, was living in some little town in Ohio called Waynesville with his wife Becky. He taught at the local high school. Patti still lived in the Quad Cities and was teaching kindergarten but lived in her own apartment. Jim was on a VA plan at Iowa State and Tad had gone off to New York to some art school. Apparently, those goofy superhero cartoons he spent his childhood doodling had been good enough to get him a scholarship... to learn to draw goofy superhero cartoons, but artfully.

The December days and nights that year were like December days when I was young—they moved like molasses. Except for different reasons. When we were kids, I couldn't wait for Christmas. This year I couldn't wait for spring. March would bring my birthday and the beginning of baseball practice. My sixteenth birthday. Getting my driver's license. Getting some friggin' freedom. But in December, it looked like it would never get here. Day after day of the drudgery of class and homework, made more painful by the fact that the basketball team was undefeated and Stone was being celebrated as the next coming of Larry Bird. What a pain in my butt. The only upside was the age advantage Olsen had enjoyed since we had known him had disappeared and he was riding the bench on the JV team. Sweet justice. He was still an asshole.

By Saturday, December 16th, the day of our Christmas dance, the bottom had fallen out of the temperatures. Normally, we'd see thirties, maybe forties as highs. The high that day was like seven degrees, the low way down below zero. We were all scrambling to find a warm enough coat to go over our fancy dresses and suits. I was wearing my army surplus parka, the winter camouflage one, a brilliant fashion statement if I do say so myself. The Christmas dance was the last dress up event until prom so for us it was a pretty big deal. I'd given up my promise to avoid dances, probably because I was bored out of my skull.

Stone deemed Nancy and me cool enough to share his table so at least we weren't relegated to the loser side of the room. And the food was good, mostly because the moms had pitched in to supply tons of Christmas cookies. The chorus came on the stage and did excerpts from its Christmas concert, thankfully cut way down 'cause a guy can only stand so much *Adestes Fideles* and *Silent Night*. There was no dancing and only a smattering of applause.

After the chorus cleared the stage, it darkened and Monsignor Morgan, our principal, came to the microphone and tapped on it. Big Al, as we called him, cleared his throat and announced, in that high pitched voice which always made us all stifle giggles, "Tonight we have a special treat for you. I'd like to introduce a new band from right here at St. Aloysius. Ladies and gentlemen, Blake's Tyger." The stage went dark.

When the lights came up, you coulda knocked me off my chair with a feather. There was Charlie, along with his friend Shawn, the goth girl with the pretty voice, Regan, and some freckle-faced girl I'd never seen before sitting behind a set of drums. They immediately started playing Phil Collins' *Another Day in Paradise.* Everyone applauded. They were good, very good. Shawn and Charlie on guitar, goth girl on keyboard and the new kid banging the drums. They were all dressed in black but only goth girl had on black makeup.

Over the next 45 minutes they played a range of songs, from the Beatles to Madonna, with enough slow songs to make the girls happy. After they finished *What a Wonderful World,* which had gotten everyone on the dance floor, the spotlight came down onto Shawn's face and he introduced the band members. When the spot went on Charlie, he smiled and dipped his head. I could tell he was really enjoying himself. I felt compelled to whistle and yell out his name. It made him grin.

After the introductions, Shawn said, "This next song was written by Regan, with a little help on the music from *moi.*" He stepped back and the spot went on Regan, who kept her eyes downcast. She sang slowly, in that remarkable voice of hers, every note a little bell, every break, a little hurt.

"My folks said don't you worry
Other kids can be so mean
And you won't have this problem
By the time you are a teen.

133

I got older and kept trying
but the stammering remained
And the meanness of the little kids
Became a whole lot less restrained.

I learned to keep quiet
To retreat into a shell
Kept my head down in a silence
Suffered in my own pure hell.

Found in music a new group
Of others with more pains
A total band of misfits
With anguish in their veins.

Oh the ghost of my childhood
So happy and carefree
But all my black
Won't bring it back.

But all my black
Won't bring it back."

The room went completely dark. The crowd, which had moved both closer and farther away from the stage, was silent. We didn't know how to react. The stage remained dark for at least a whole minute and when the lights came back up, the band had changed clothes, somehow. The guys had on red bowties and the girls both had on red, Regan in a dress and the drummer, Beckett, in a suit. They all wore Santa hats. They immediately went into a rendition of Brenda Lee's *Jingle Bell Rock*. Everyone cheered.

Everyone, I noticed, except Scott Olsen and his little gang of pricks. It was obvious Scott was not happy with Charlie and his success. I saw him point at Charlie and say something to his minions. They laughed. They were a motley bunch, just the kind of losers who would worship Scott. There was a fat roly-poly kid named Bruce Creager, who everybody called Chubbs. Slow would have been a step up for him, both physically and mentally. The skinny shrimp with the acne, who we called Pimps, short for pimples, was John Peterson. Around seventh grade he developed the worst case of acne anyone ever saw. It got worse as puberty hit full stride. The quartet was completed with a hulking black dude named Johnny Cooper. Nobody called him anything but Sir.

The following Monday, Father Bouvier sent word for me to report to his office during my study hall period. Father was the school's guidance counselor, in addition to teaching religion. I figured it was gonna be his annual run at convincing me to go into the priesthood, like he did every year with every male student. I asked him once if he did the same thing with girls. You know, try to make them into nuns. "Nah," he told me. "They'd have to be crazy to do that. And we have enough crazies in the church now as it is."

"Have a seat," he ordered. He was using his official tone. I obliged. "Tell me, Winston, you've been friends with Charles Settler for a long time, right?"

"Yessir."

"I need to know a little about his past," the priest continued. "What do you know about his family, about his childhood?" Apparently my body language told him I didn't want to answer. "Cutter, think of this as the confessional. What you say here stays between us, okay?"

"But it isn't, is it?"

He smiled. "No, it isn't, so I guess I'm asking you to trust me."

"What do you want to know? And why?"

"Charlie is very bright. Very. His test scores are chart topping. His shop teachers say he knows more about mechanics and tools and motors than they do. But he isn't in any college prep classes. Why is that? Does he have a bad family life? Don't they care about what happens to him? What don't we know that we should?"

"I dunno."

Father Bouvier stared at me. Long enough that I started fidgeting in my seat.

"So nothing, eh?" He paused. "I was just thinking that maybe he didn't realize what he could do, what he could be. What do you think?"

"I think he's a great guy who's never gotten a break." Father raised his eyebrows. I thought about it a minute. "It stays here, right?" He nodded.

"Charlie's dad wasn't his real dad. He had a different dad than all of his brothers and sisters and his fake dad beat him. A lot. He even broke his arm once and ruined the best pitcher I ever saw. When his family moved from DeWitt, his fake dad didn't want to take him with them and they sent him to live with an aunt. Who isn't even a real aunt. He's mostly taking care of himself. I think the guy beat his mom as well. And Charlie's a great guy. He got screwed when they kicked him off the basketball team. He used to stutter a lot and kids made fun of him. I think he's afraid people won't like him." It all came out in a rush and I hoped to God I wasn't screwing him over as well.

The priest asked a few more questions about his elementary teachers and how I got to know him and so on. Then he told me he was going to try to get Charlie interested in going to college and maybe I should suggest it to Charlie as well. I got up to leave.

As I got to the door, he said, "Wait a second, Cutter. I've got one more thing."

"Yeah?"

"I hear you use the phrase 'Christ in a handbasket' and that you have told other teachers I taught you that."

I felt my face flush. "Sorry."

"Well, in the future please feel free to NOT credit me with it, okay?"

I felt like I should repeat my confessional line, "Bless me, Father, for I have sinned..." but instead I uttered the priest's, "Go. And sin no more." Though I was pretty sure I would. Father Bouvier bowed his head and sighed but I knew he was smiling.

Three days later was the last day of class before Christmas break. Normally by this time of year I would be practically peeing my pants with excitement. Now I just sulked around the house and pouted until Christmas Eve. Everyone was home by then and I finally kinda got into the mood. We had a big dinner and went to midnight mass. Most of my friends were there and there was snow on the ground and it was still very cold and it felt, I dunno, really good. Just before mass started, I was looking around and saw Charlie in the back, by himself. I waved him to come sit with us.

Both my mom and dad gave him a big hug and Mom asked him if he was having Christmas with his family. He shook his head and Mom hugged him again and said to Dad, "Henry, Charlie is coming home with us tonight to spend Christmas with us."

It made me happy and sad at the same time and I whispered to my mom, "I'm really sorry for acting like an asshole the last few weeks. Can we give Charlie some of my presents tomorrow morning? You know, so he has something to open."

"Cutter, don't use that word, especially in church." Then she smiled and hugged me and said, "Yes, I think that would be very nice of you. Very nice."

It would have been like the perfect Christmas except for my taking Jim's asshole advice. I got Nancy a tee shirt that said, "St. Aloysius High School Where Fun Goes to Die." She had gotten me a nice sweater and tickets to see the stage production of *Little Shop of Horrors*. Boy, had I misread what she was thinking about us. She tried to act pleased but I could tell I had really screwed up. Thanks, Jim. Thanks a bunch.

CHAPTER TWENTY-FOUR

Charlie called Regan right after Christmas and invited her for some holiday ice cream at Lagomarcino's in the East Village. She was already in a booth when he showed up. "Hey, Stranger, long time, no see," she said and smiled. They had not been together since the night of their concert. "How was your Christmas? Santa good to you?"

"A-a-a-as good as he always is," he smiled and paused. "Actually, better. You?" Before she could answer, he added, "What's with the clothes? Where's your black?" Regan was wearing a dark brown sweater over winter white pants, brown boots and a white ski hat.

"I dunno. I kinda decided I liked not wearing black. My mom was so excited she got me like five new outfits for Christmas. You think I look okay?"

Charlie grinned, "You look terrific. B-b-b-beautiful."

"Shawn doesn't like it as much as the black look. I told him I'd still wear that too. Though it's his fault. He was the one who wanted me to change into that red dress at the concert." She rolled her eyes. "But he did get me this for Christmas." She held up the small diamond pendant around her neck. "It's from Tiffany's."

"Nice." But he didn't smile.

She went on, "Did you see your family for Christmas?"

Now he frowned. "No." He said nothing else.

"I'm sorry," she said, worried she had said the wrong thing. "You said Santa was good to you, though. Did they send presents?"

"I got one from my mom and all the brothers and sisters sent cards. The day was okay because Cutter's parents invited me to spend Christmas with them." He paused, then went on, "I really like his family. His mom and dad have always been really nice to me."

The ice cream sundaes they ordered had arrived and they busied themselves with eating. Charlie surreptitiously eyed the pendant. "Is that a diamond?" She nodded. They finished eating in silence.

After they ate and he bought her a piece of chocolate, Charlie asked Regan, "Father Bouvier had me in his office last week and thinks I should be taking college prep classes. You think I should?"

"I dunno. Why aren't you?"

He thought for a minute. "I guess 'cause I like motors and stuff. And there ain't no way I could ever go to college."

"Why not? You get good grades and you're plenty smart."

He rubbed his first two fingers with his thumb. "No moola. Fixin' lawn mowers doesn't make me a fortune, ya know."

She smiled at him. Then reached over and took his mechanic's stained hand in both of hers. "For a smart guy, you can be a real idiot. Loans, scholarships. Work/study programs. Junior college to start if need be. Yeah, Dopey, you should switch to college prep." She squeezed his hand 'til he flinched and then dropped it.

"We're halfway through our sophomore year. How could I get caught up?"

"Caught up? With what? You take English and history and I'm sure your mechanical drawing is as good as plane geometry. You got nothing to get caught up with. Look, if Shawn and Cutter and Stone and even Olsen can do it, it'll be a snap for you." She stood up and put on her coat. "See you in biology class, which I guarantee will be more interesting than Sister Beverly's Gen Science class." She turned and walked out into the blowing snow. He watched her walk away. His smile hurt.

****

140

I had my head down, trying to finish the last three homework questions before old lady Polly showed up for plane geometry. It was part of a running battle she and I had, though I knew she secretly really liked me. It had started when early in the school year I had walked into her classroom with my shirttail hanging out. Or tried to. She put her arm across the doorway, stopped me and said, in as gruff a voice as she could muster (which wasn't very), "You know you can't come in here with your shirt untucked." So I made a big show of laying my backpack on the floor, then unzipping my pants to tuck in my shirt, knowing that was not what she intended. She turned red (score one for Cutter) and barked, "You're out of class for a week. Go to Father Powers' office." Scott Powers was the assistant principal. When I told Father why I was there, he laughed and told me he didn't care where I went but to get out of his office. I wandered the halls for third period the whole next week.

Anyway, I was trying to finish the homework and this voice says, "Hey, C-c-c-c-utter, you need some help? Math too hard for you?" I looked up and saw Charlie smiling at me.

"What are you doing here? Lost?" I smiled back.

"Sorta. I switched to college prep classes and they moved me from mechanical drawing to this class." He paused. "Need me to show you how to draw a triangle?" He laughed and sat at the desk next to mine. I finished the last problem as he got out his notebook and took out his schedule card. When Mrs. Polly came in, he took it up to her and explained why he was there.

When he got back to his seat, I grabbed the card from his hand to find that his class schedule was, except for two classes, the same as mine. He was taking French I at the same time I had French II and he had kept his automotive mechanics class the period I took typing. I leaned over and whispered (since Mrs. Polly would kick me out again for talking in class), "Hey, looks like the dynamic duo is back together. Just like Mr. Turner's fifth grade class."

In fact, it was a lot like fifth grade. Charlie blew right by me, grades-wise, and even got moved up to French II before year's end. Seems his friend the goth girl was a language wiz and tutored him to catch up. In fact, the only course I scored better in was English.

Winter seemed to last forever but March and my birthday finally arrived. It took two tries, but by late April I had my temp driver's license and baseball was in full swing. So to speak. Funny, in looking back, I realize there was this rhythm to high school. We were all waiting for something, anticipating something, biding our time. I suppose like someone in jail, knowing that someday, somewhere way out in the future there was freedom, but for now, it was just this rhythmic passage of days. Slash another tally mark on the wall, inch closer to an ever-receding finish line.

The thing is, though, they trick you. High school is supposed to be preparation for college and life. Turns out it prepares you for life the way batting practice prepares you for a ball game. At batting practice, there is this rhythm of the coach throwing you ball after ball, same speed, same location, same pitch, over and over. You begin to feel the rhythm in your bat. Your body sways gently waiting for the next pitch and your swing is effortless, mindless. High school days were like that. Your being just kind of swayed with the rhythm of each school day, week, term and year.

Then you get into a game. This guy on the mound, 60 feet, 6 inches away from you, has one goal. Make you look bad. Trick you with an unanticipated pitch, change the speed of the pitches and, most frustrating of all, change the time between pitches. Two come real fast and hard, the next one you have to wait for and the final slow one strikes you out. You can find no rhythm, no discernable pace. You bear down, and if you are any good, about one third of the time you get a hit. And that's only if you are good.

Post high school does the same thing to you. There is no pattern to what comes at you, no anticipating the speed or power or meaning. You spend those four years planning how you are going to play the game, how you are going to get hit after hit, how you will be the hero and win the game and then there are all those guys whose only *raison d'être* is to make you look bad. That is, if you actually make it to game time. Some don't.

J. Woodburn's wife, the ever delightful Deborah Varner, and I have had several conversations about the impact of high school on the rest of our lives. About how four crummy years define how you see yourself for many years to come. How you try to correct for what you perceived were your inadequacies in your teen years, how you try to recapture the small glories you won then. How the way you thought others perceived you was your measuring stick of self-worth, even though, truth be told, most were so busy feeling the same things you were feeling, they didn't even notice you.

I have been struck, especially over the last few years, by the things others remember you for and you have no recollection of those events or comments or niceties or slights. And vice versa. The things your fellow high schoolers said or did that you have carried for years, and they have no memory of them. At all. Ms. Varner has assured me we all feel that way. And that there is no way to protect our children from feeling those things.

Throughout the remainder of our sophomore year, the group of us who would stay together over the rest of high school coalesced. Oddly, though maybe not oddly at all, it grew around Charlie. Besides him and me, there was my main guy, Stone and his girlfriend Alexandra, Shawn, Regan, Lynne, Alan, Beckett and my brother Tim. You'll notice Nancy didn't make the cut. Though, in fact, she's the one who cut me loose. Smart girl. Tim only made it because he started dating Beckett.

Most of us got summer jobs, saved some money, spent weekend nights hanging out as a group or in various combinations thereof. Blake's Tyger got a regular gig at a place in the East Village and at the end of summer, Shawn and Charlie had us all over for a big party. Where I had my first whole beer. It was an Old Style. As Hemingway might say, "The beer, it was cold. It was strong. It made us feel like men. We weren't."

CHAPTER TWENTY-FIVE

"Hey, Cutter," Stone yelled from down the hall. "D'ja hear? After school. Student parking lot. Olsen is fighting Alan Johnson."

"Beanpole?"

"Don'cha wanna watch?"

"Not really. I don't need to see Olsen beat up another kid."

"N-n-not a big deal. Won't happen. No way is Olsen winning." Charlie's voice came from behind me.

"You're kidding. Johnson is so damn skinny he won't have a chance. Besides, Olsen is just plain mean."

"Wager?" Charlie asked.

By now Stone had reached us by our lockers. "I'll take some of that bet, even if Cutter won't. Johnson's a good ball player, but I've seen little guys shove him around and he never shoves back."

I eyed Charlie. "What makes you so sure Alan won't get his ass kicked?"

Charlie smiled. "Because I trained him." Stone and I both laughed.

"Yeah," I told him, "we'll take the bet. Ten bucks? Each."

"You're on."

"Last chance to back out."

Stone shook his head and said, "Nah. We're good."

"Just outta curiosity," I asked. "How did you train him?"

Now Charlie grinned. "I shared my expert knowledge of p-p-p-p-pugilism with him." He paused to enjoy our giggles. Then, "Oh, and you know how Olsen always gets in your face before he throws a punch? I told Alan that as soon as Olsen moves in on him, throw an uppercut to his jaw. You know, like Butch Cassidy did with the crotch kick. Don't give him a chance to hit you."

It went down exactly like Charlie described it. Best ten dollars I ever spent. And we all swore to the powers that be, that Olsen had thrown the first punch. Alan only got reprimanded and put on in-school probation. Olsen got the same punishment, on accounta of most of his group of misfits swore Alan hit first. Except he of the dim wit, Chubbs. Chubbs said he couldn't remember.

A few days later, Shawn was walking toward his locker, not paying attention and Olsen threw him a shoulder as he passed. Shawn was not expecting it and ended up sitting on his ass next to the wall. He barked at Olsen's back, "Careful Scotty, or I'll sic Beanpole Johnson on you again," and laughed. Olsen spun around and came back.

"Fuck you, rich kid. Johnson threw a sucker punch and he'll pay for it."

Shawn was still sitting on the floor. "I doubt it, not with Charlie Settler in his corner."

Shawn pulled himself up and saw Scott's face had darkened. He realized he probably shouldn't have said that and flinched when Olsen put a finger in his face and said, "You tell your buddy Settler I'll make sure to pay him back as well."

When Shawn told us about it, Charlie just smiled and told Shawn not to worry about it. He finished by saying, "O-o-o-o-o, I'm shakin' in my boots." It was the first time I ever saw Charlie make fun of his own stuttering.

A few days later we were all hanging out at Shawn's when his dad came in and announced, "Hey Shawn, I talked to the vice president of admissions at Berklee today and she said you need to get your application in ASAP. They do auditions in the spring and it's on a first come, first served basis. I don't want to have to remind you again."

Shawn waved his hand at his dad, irritated like, and said. "Yeah, yeah, yeah. I'll get it done. Don't worry about it." His dad shook his head and left without saying anything more.

Stone got a confused look on his face and asked Shawn, "You're going to Berkeley? What, to become a hippie? That sounds like something more up Regan's alley." Regan laughed.

"No, you idjit. Berklee College of Music in Boston." He paused when he saw us all look confused. "It's like one of the best music schools around. As good as Julliard. Just not as famous." Another pause. "So where are you guys going to college?"

We all just stared at him. Not so much because we had never heard of Berklee, though we hadn't, but because none of us had really thought about it. We all just kinda shrugged our shoulders and finally Stone said, "I dunno. Wherever I get the best b-ball scholarship. Like probably Duke." He grinned. He had actually heard, already, as a sophomore, from Augustana and Drake. Not exactly powerhouse basketball programs, but he claimed the big schools would come calling when he took St. Al to the state championship. We didn't hold our breath.

It kinda made me think about what kind of scholarship Charlie might have gotten if he hadn't been kicked out of sports. Damn that Olsen.

That night at the dinner table, I asked my parents about where they thought I should go to school. My dad stopped midchew but before he could respond, Tim piped up with "the state school for dorks and dweebs." I threw a roll at him and Dad threatened to banish us from the table. Neither of my parents had gone to college—Dad because he had to go to work and Mom because she wanted to stay where Dad was. But they were pretty adamant about us all going. Every one of my older siblings had gone to college, even Jim after his three year stint in the military. Chris had just started at the University of Indiana 'cause he was some kind of science whiz.

My dad asked, "So, Cutter, any idea where you would like to go? What do you think you want to study?"

I thought for a couple of minutes. I didn't really want to have to do any work, ever, and tried to think of what I liked in high school. "I dunno. Maybe English."

Dad rolled his eyes. "Yeah, lot of demand for people who study English. You think maybe you can get a job talking?"

My mom interceded. "You know, University of Iowa has one of the best English and writing programs in the country." It was my turn to roll my eyes. No one wanted to go to Iowa. It'd be like being a townie. Even worse than Augustana. Though I knew where I would get to go would be largely determined by what, if any, scholarships I might get. My mom went on, "Maybe you should pick a few schools and go visit them. Henry, do you think you should take Cutter, and maybe Tim, around to just check out some schools? You know, places you could drive to."

"Can Charlie go with us? I don't think he's ever even been to a college?"

"Why, sure. That'd be fine."

The next day, I told the guys about it and asked Charlie if he wanted to go with us. Regan asked, "Hey, what about me? Don't I get to go?" Then, Lynne and Beckett wanted to go and Shawn said if it was a party he needed to be there as well. Long story short, long story which includes lots of parent to parent conversations, it was settled. Shawn's parents rented us a big old GMC nine passenger van, the other parents (except Charlie's, of course) kicked in money and we asked Father Bouvier, the guidance counselor, what he thought. He added one he wanted Charlie to visit.

In mid-October, with my parents as chaperones, we set out to visit Iowa, University of Wisconsin, Northwestern, University of Chicago, University of

Illinois, Purdue, Illinois State and Northern Illinois. Iowa State got rejected on accounta it was the wrong direction and who would ever want to go there. It was, we all knew, the dork and nerd school. We had argued over what schools to visit, but we knew we wanted to do a little partying in Mad City and in Chicago, so we chose U of Chicago and U of Wisconsin to insure that, then each of us picked one more. Tim and I tried to warn our parents not to be embarrassing, though we knew it would be to no avail.

We started planning and quickly got into arguments about where to go when, how much time to spend at each, whether it would be a drop by visit on our own or if we should contact the colleges to get tours. After about two hours of arguing, Mom stepped in and appointed Lynne, Regan and herself to do all the planning. She let Dad pick the driving routes. The rest of us got to get the road trip snacks.

One evening a few days before the trip, Mom said, "Cutter, I really like your friend Regan. Why don't you ask her out? She seems like a great girl?"

Before I could answer, Dad grumped, "What was wrong with that Nancy girl? I really liked her."

I ignored him then told Mom, "Yeah, Regan is pretty cool. But she's dating Shawn and I think Charlie really likes her as well. I'd have to get in line."

Dad grumped again, "Cutter, you're probably better off single." I wish he had lived long enough to meet Rachel.

CHAPTER TWENTY-SIX

The schedule Regan and Mom decided on would be the northern schools first, then swing south, leaving on Thursday morning and returning Tuesday evening. Before the day even started, enough of us whined about having to go to Iowa City, we dropped it from the schedule. Mom was not pleased because she had arranged for me to meet with some big time English professor and told me something to the effect that, "You'll be sorry you missed this opportunity." I wasn't.

We first drove to Northern Illinois and spent like a total of two hours there. It was unanimous that NIU would be the last option anyone would take and then maybe only after Scott County Community College and Trade School wouldn't take you. We arrived in Madison late afternoon and after a little driving tour of the city, checked into our motel and had pizza. We finally convinced the parents we would be okay on our own and we headed down to State Street which is where the cool college kids all hang out. It was the first time I ever got really excited about going to college. These kids were definitely way cool.

The next day we had the obligatory tours and listened to the blah, blah, blah until our heads were about to explode. The last part of the tour was a visit to Camp Randall Stadium and we ended the afternoon on the Union Terrace overlooking Lake Mendota. Right then and there, I decided that I wanted to be a Badger for sure. This is where I was going to college. It was just too cool. One of the guys who was a tour guide asked us, "So, you're sticking around for the game tomorrow, right?"

Lynne perked right up. "Can we get tickets?"

The guide laughed and shook his head. "As if. We're playing Michigan and they're like number two in the country right now. Besides, only fart-knockers go to the actual game." Apparently that was a term for dorks, but what did we know? We lived in the QC. Of course, we were cool enough not to ask. "Nah," the guide went on, "What you wanna do is go to the fifth quarter." He explained to us that most students went to Camp Randall at the end of the game and got in for free and the band came on the field and played and it was like a seventy thousand person party.

After much convincing of the parents, we got to go to the fifth quarter and it was everything the guy told us. And a bag of chips. The really funny thing was the Badgers had gotten their asses handed to them 41 to 3 and nobody cared. The party still went on. Charlie turned to me, grinning, and said, "I-i-i-i-if this is college, count me in. It would be so c-c-cool to go here." By the time we left Madison, we pretty much all agreed.

Early Sunday morning, we drove down to Evanston and did a self-tour of Northwestern and all us kids decided it was kind of a mistake on the lake. It rated above NIU, but barely. It certainly wasn't any Wisconsin. Sunday afternoon I got my first ride on the L. We had checked into the Holiday Inn in Evanston and Mom quickly shepherded us down to the Dempster Station on the purple line where we got the train downtown. Dad stayed behind, claiming he needed to rest, though we all knew he just wanted to watch the Bears play the dreaded Packers on TV.

I gotta admit, I was pretty scared by the whole train to downtown thing but excited too. Mostly, I was amazed my mom knew how to do this. "How do you know so much about this stuff?" I asked her.

She smiled and said to Lynne and Regan, "Cutter thinks my life didn't start until the day he was born. He can't accept that I got to do things without him." She and my friends laughed. Ha ha. Some friends.

The Art Institute was overwhelming. I was really beginning to feel like a hick. Especially since Regan and Shawn were used to big cities and, apparently, my mom was as well. I didn't let on like I was scared or anything so the other guys wouldn't catch on. I did see Beckett holding on to Tim's hand like crazy, which meant he had to act cool as well. Funny, acting like you're not intimidated is part of actually not being intimidated. As long as you have your mom along to protect you, I guess.

The art museum did not improve my comfort level. I had seen lots of photos of paintings in books, sure, it wasn't like I was a total cretin. But this was the first time I had ever seen the actual paintings. Right there in front of me. And some of them were huge. I loved *Sunday Afternoon on the Island of La Grande Jatte*. You could get close enough to see the little dots of paint. Like the guy had just done it. I tried to act all nonchalant and all, until Charlie whispered to me he was feeling exactly the same thing. I coulda hugged him. I didn't.

We'd been at the museum for a couple of hours when Shawn took mom aside and whispered to her. She called us all together. "Shawn would like to take us over to the Palmer House for ice cream. His treat. If you all want to go."

"Is the Palmer House Red's grandparents or something?" Tim asked.

Lynne rolled her eyes. "No, duh. It's like a famous hotel. And don't call me Red." I could tell Tim felt like a rube as well.

We all wanted to go. I'd been to the Blackhawk in Davenport and figured this would be about the same. It wasn't. The lobby was like the size of a football field. Everyone was dressed up. Except us, of course. Shawn said not to worry though. They'd still take our money. I eventually came to understand that was a pretty important lesson. After we had sundaes, he suggested we go to the top of the Sears Tower. As I stood looking out over Lake Michigan, I thought, "Screw Madison. This is where I'm going to college." And our visit to the University of Chicago the next day sealed the deal. I felt at home there. It was perfect.

Monday morning we drove the three hours down to Purdue where we met with an engineering graduate student who was to take us on a tour of the college. It was a pretty warm fall day and it was good to be back in the country and see trees with fall color. So we were moderately excited to walk the campus. Just as we were leaving, a guy with thick glasses and about a dozen pens in a pocket protector called out to Charlie.

"Excuse me, but is one of you Charles Settler?" Charlie raised his hand. "Great," the guy went on, "Professor Jakubs has asked if you would mind giving up your tour and maybe chatting with us for a couple of hours." When Charlie didn't respond, the guy turned to my folks and asked, "Would that be all right?"

My dad spoke first. "Sure. Charlie, why don't you talk with the professor? You might be able to ask some questions about the university and about engineering, you know, to see if you might be interested in that as something to study." Charlie remained mute. Dad asked, "Would you like me to stay with you?"

Charlie slowly shook his head. "N-n-n-nah," and then to the young man, "Okay, I-i-i-i would like to talk to the professor." He turned to Mom and asked, "Is that okay with you guys?" She smiled and nodded and Charlie turned to follow the guy.

Regan quickly grabbed his arm and gave him a hug. She whispered, loud enough for us all to hear, "Good luck!" We headed out for a tour.

About one, we finished the tour and our graduate student took us to a dining hall and she told us we could help ourselves to whatever we wanted. Cool. We loaded up our trays and had just sat down when Charlie walked in with this insanely tall, middle aged guy who looked like he was left over from the 60s, right down to his bell-bottomed jeans which had more patches than original denim. He must have been six eight or nine, round wire rim glasses, a long wispy mustache and hair down to his shoulders. He would have looked downright scary had it not been for the huge grin he wore. Charlie looked serious, almost stern.

"Mr. and Mrs. Williams, I'm Jack Jakubs. I'm the dean of the College of Engineering." He stuck out his hand, first to Mom and then to Dad. "Charlie here tells me he doesn't live with his folks, but that I should talk to you in their place. Is that okay?"

"Well," my dad said slowly, "we can't legally speak for him, but he's kinda part of the family, so yeah, we would love to hear what you have to say about him." My mom smiled and nodded agreement. Charlie blushed.

"Charlie, you sure it's okay?" the old hippie asked.

"S-s-sure, Dr. Jakubs," Charlie answered.

The professor looked all of us kids over and turned to my folks. "Charlie is quite a young man, as I'm sure you know. We talked a while about his interest in machines and then we spent about an hour giving him a few, um, tests. I gotta tell you, your Mr. Settler here is an exceptional talent. We have never seen such an aptitude for engineering. And we're one of the best schools in the nation in engineering." All of us were staring at Charlie by this time. "We want him to come here. And we want him bad enough that right now, if he'll commit to joining us, we are offering him a full ride scholarship. Tuition, out-of-state fees, room and board, books and a monthly stipend, along with a job working in one of our labs." He paused just long enough to see the stunned reaction on all of our faces and went on, "So, Charlie, what do you say?"

CHAPTER TWENTY-SEVEN

A few weeks later, Charlie and Regan were sitting on the gym bleachers during lunch hour, watching about twenty freshmen fight over one basketball, trying to outdo each other just to shoot a basket where their high school heroes played. Regan laughed.

"What?" Charlie wanted to know.

"Do you think those kids are trying to be Stone? You know, dreams of being the hero of the game and being popular? If only they knew."

"What?" Charlie repeated.

"That he's just a regular guy. Who happens to be a good athlete." She paused and looked at him, then took his hand in hers. "And they have no idea how much better you would have been. And how unimportant it is."

Charlie smiled and said nothing.

"So why did you tell that dean at Purdue you'd think about it?"

Charlie laughed. "It was kind of a joke. I'd already told him I would accept the scholarship. He asked me to promise, then told me, 'Charles, I want you to remember your commitment to Purdue when schools like MIT and CalTech come offering you scholarships.' I promised I would."

"I've decided I'm going to go back east, back to Philadelphia, for school. I still miss it," she told him.

"To be nearer to Shawn?"

She was quiet a long time. Finally, "No." She paused. "Not really." She paused again. "Maybe some." He stared at the would-be basketball stars.

****

After our trip to visit colleges, school seemed to change a lot. Like what had been the most important part of our lives now didn't seem to matter all that much. We went to class, we hung out, we went on dates and worked some part-time jobs. Shawn and Charlie's band still played sometimes at our dances and in the East Village and, of course, Stone was back into basketball. It wasn't that I felt edgy or nervous or anything, just impatient for it all to be over. In fact, the year would have been a total bust had it not been for the famous Stone Socks Massacre.

The basketball team was picked to be a state title contender. Of course, St. Al was, is, a small school so it wasn't like we were up against the big schools. Still, we had some stiff competition. Stone was the star, Alan Johnson the big man in the middle. He was still six eight, but he'd put on about 25 pounds and, after taking down Olsen in the infamous one punch fight, he had toughened up and no one was pushing him around. Had Charlie been able to play, there was not a team in the state, maybe the whole Midwest, which could have beaten them.

They lost their first game. Badly. Bad enough the Quad City Times banner sports headline on Sunday morning read: "Saint Aloysius Stumbles" followed by "Has Stone Miller Lost It?" The following Wednesday we played DeWitt High School and I got to see some of my old group, the squad. In fact, Randy was on their team and Booger showed up to watch. Booger had turned into a dork but it was okay. I introduced him as my country bumpkin friend and let him sit with us. Our whole group was there, except Charlie.

As the team was introduced before the game, a few of the kids started chanting, "Loser, loser." when Stone was introduced. You could see his face turn red and he kept staring at the floor. He then went out and played his heart out. He scored 32 of the team's 52 points, had half dozen rebounds and five steals. St. Al won handily. The same kids who had chanted "Loser" were now chanting "Stone, Stone."

After the game, as the team sat in the locker room grinning and high fiving, Stone stood up on one of the benches and held up a pair of socks. He told everyone to quiet down and announced, "These are my lucky socks. I am not going to wash them as long as we keep winning." He then threw them at Alan's head.

Five weeks later, they had won 11 straight games and no one on the team was washing their socks. They had weekly contests to see whose socks smelled the worst. Turned out Alan's stank so bad, they had to have a contest for the second worst smelling socks. Alan claimed his secret was he didn't wash his feet either.

News spread throughout the school and pretty soon all the guys were not washing their socks in a show of solidarity. Then Lynne got the cheerleaders to join in and pretty soon, not one student in the entire school was washing their socks. In some classes the aroma was so pungent it brought tears to your eyes.

Our principal, Monsignor Big Al Morgan, had had enough. He called an assembly.

"Ladies and gentlemen, you may notice that the air in this hall is barely breathable. Frankly the stench is overpowering. And it is my understanding that it is all of your faults. Starting today, no one will be permitted to come to school unless they're wearing fresh clean socks and shoes. No One. That especially applies to the basketball team. While we all applaud their winning so many games and appreciate the honor they are bringing to our school, I must remind you that those wins have nothing to do with how smelly socks are. In fact, that belief goes as far as superstition and you know that superstition and superstitious practices are a sin as far as the church is concerned. So it stops today. Dismissed." With that he left the stage and you could hear the groans around the entire room.

We lost our next game and Big Al had to go into hiding. The magic was over. After that loss, the team returned to its winning ways and would ultimately make it into the regional finals before losing again.

A couple of weeks after the clean socks loss, I stopped into Father Bouvier's office to pick up some info on the SATs.

"Your boy Stone Miller is having himself a great season," Father Dave said.

"Yep. Would have been even better if Big Al hadn't screwed things up," I told him. Father Dave laughed. I asked him, "So what is the big deal with this whole superstition thing? It was working. Why is it a sin or whatever? Seems stupid to me."

"I think the monsignor was just trying to get rid of the smell. You know how superstitions work. Folks believe in some magic that has no place in the realm of reason or science. 'We did something and then something good happened. If we do it again, then some new good will happen for us.' There doesn't have to be any cause and effect relationship. You know, like believing that a volcano is a god and the volcano erupts when he gets mad. So if a virgin would make a man happy and not mad, it should work for a god as well. Let's just throw the volcano god a virgin to stop an eruption."

It was my turn to laugh. "I get it. But what was the whole thing about being a sin? That's just ridiculous. What's the harm in a little fun?"

Father Bouvier turned serious. "Ah, there's the rub, as they say. The church doesn't want any competition. You know, in believing in things which may or may not exist. Which might be but aren't provable. I mean, where would it stop? If praying to our god doesn't work, let's pray to another god. Well, crap, Cutter, the church would lose all its power. It gets to dictate what the superstitions are. It's the only way it can retain its power. And its money."

I thought about it. "Then aren't all religions superstition?"

"Yep. And they happen just like the basketball socks thing. A few people believe in something unprovable, then more people join in because they see the opportunity for some kind of personal reward, like life everlasting or other such nonsense. And voila, a superstition becomes a belief. And there are always those who will see a way to make money and get power over people by encouraging those superstitions. And that, Son, is where religion comes from. Though I'll deny I ever told you that," and he laughed again.

You know, when I sat down to write this story, we were in the middle of the COVID epidemic. Shortly after I started writing, a group of vaccines were released and made available at no cost to people. They were scientifically developed with techniques which took decades to create. Their safety was studied. And studied again. They were effective, highly effective. And yet people, a lot of whom also believed strongly in the superstition of religion, also chose to believe in some magic other than the science of the vaccines. I don't get it. Life is tough enough without having to believe in someone else's superstitions. I guess Jesus wasn't kidding when he said, "These are my Sheep." To this day, I suffer not the self-righteous self-indulgences of organized religion and its followers. The whole experience kinda fell under the Law of Unintended Consequences.

At any rate, the Midwest religion of high school basketball continued, the tried and true bastion against the utter dreariness of Iowa winter. We probably should have gone to the state finals, but two weeks before the end of the regular season, my buddy Scott Olsen undercut Stone during a practice scrimmage as Stone went in for a lay-up. Stone's head bounced off the floor like an over inflated basketball. He wasn't knocked out, but they took him to the hospital where they diagnosed a severe concussion and ordered Stone out of the game for ten days. The team, though it kept winning, was never the same that season, even after Stone returned.

The only bright side was Olsen got thrown off the team. As the season progressed his fortunes had steadily fallen. He had gone from starter to sixth man to butt-splinter-picking bench rider. He made no effort to hide his belief that Stone was responsible, and even more oddly, that somehow Charlie had helped screw him over. He had made the fatal mistake of telling another teammate that he would knock Stone down a peg or two when he got the chance. Bye-bye, Olsen.

CHAPTER TWENTY-EIGHT

Spring brought baseball, golf, the prom and the itch to be out of school. The ball team did okay. I had a good year. Even made second team all-league. But baseball was like pretty much everything else high school. Boring. In fact, it worked out it was my last time ever on a sports team, unless you count the city golf league when I lived in Columbus. There is a lot to be said for not doing something so long the joy goes out of it.

On the up side, while I was furtively casting about for a prom date, Stone told me his cousin Erica Denner was back on the market and she'd go with me...maybe. Good ole' Erica. Big boobed Erica. The make out queen. Of course, those were just my memories of her. My adolescent mind probably greatly exaggerated her eagerness to neck. I called her.

"Erica, it's me, Cutter."

"Who?" Geez, I guess my mind had exaggerated our encounters. Or maybe I was just forgettable.

"Cutter Williams. Stone's friend." Nothing. "We went out a couple of years ago, like to the movies and stuff." Still nothing.

"What did you say your name was again?" I was speechless. Finally, "Man, Cutter, I don't remember you being such a dork. You used to have a sense of humor."

"Ha ha. Veeerrrry funny, Erica." I didn't know exactly where to go from there.

"Cutter?"

"Yeah?"

"You called me. Is there something you want?"

"Well, like, I was talking with Stone the other day and he said that you might, you know..."

"Stone told me you're thinking about majoring in English at college. Based on this scintillating conversation, you may seriously want to think about taking a remedial course in it beforehand. I mean, like, you know." She paused. When I could offer no response, she said, "I've got dinner in a couple of hours. You think maybe you could get to the point of this conversation. If it, indeed, does have a point."

I felt like a total fool and knew I should turn tail and run, but before I got my wits about me, I blurted, "So you wanna go to prom? With me, I mean. Huh?"

Silence. Long enough I thought maybe she had hung up and I was starting to feel relieved. "Cutter, you are a true romantic." She launched into full-on Valley Girl Speak. "But, like, sure, Dude, that'd be, like really cool, like you know what I mean. Like even though you are, like, totally clueless." What could I say? I laughed.

"Thanks, Erica. You are, like, a real, like, gem." We both laughed. I gave her the details on the dance and invited her to dinner on Friday so we could reconnect and because I knew once she thought about it, she'd want to tell me how to dress and stuff. We hung up.

Five minutes later, the phone rang and my mom yelled up the stairs, "Cutter, phone."

"Who is it?"

Pause, then, "Erica Denner."

I took my time getting to the phone. "Yes?"

"Hey, Cutter, I've got a huge favor to ask. Do you have any friends who still need a prom date?"

"Why?"

"Because my sister is whining and my mom wants me to ask you if you can find someone to take her as well. I know," I could hear her eyes roll, "but I said I'd ask."

"Let me think about it."

A couple of days later, our group went to lunch at the Village Inn (one of the perks of being a junior was getting to go off campus for lunch) and while we were eating, Stone said, "Hey, Cutter, I hear you're taking Erica to the prom. How much did you have to pay her?"

"Are you kidding? She's paying me." Shawn laughed so hard he blew a french fry out his nose. Which of course led to more hoots of derision. But it reminded me to ask, "Charlie, who you taking to prom?"

"I'm n-n-n-not going. Costs too much and ya just get to see the same kids you see all the time anyway."

Regan reached over and grabbed his elbow, "Aw, c'mon, Charlie, we'll all go as a group, so it's not like you have to pay for a date or anything. It'll be fun. One last chance for us to all do something high schoolish together before summer break." Charlie didn't respond. "Please? For me?"

"Yeah, and it'll get me off the hook since I told Erica I'd try to get her sister Erin a date as well. I kinda remember that she's sorta cute. Though she is Stone's cousin so she's got that going against her." He said nothing. "I'll tell you what. I'm having dinner with Erica Friday. You come along and she'll bring Erin and if you don't like her, then no prom." I paused. "But Regan's right. You do have to go with us."

Shawn added, "Tell you what, Charlie, you come and I'll get my dad to get us a big ole limo to go in." By then there was a chorus of "C'mon, Charlie" until he nodded his head "yes."

"Pick me up Friday around six. I'll want Erin and Erica to see you in your cool car, you know, since you ain't much to look at..." He chucked a french fry at my face.

Friday night we met the Denner girls at the 11th Street Precinct in the East Village. Erica was still Erica, big boobs and all, but Erin had changed a lot. She wasn't just cute, she was knock-your-socks-off cute. She was a half head taller than her sister, all long limbs and grace. I immediately whispered the line from *Young Frankenstein* to Charlie, "Soitenly, you take the blonde, I'll take the one in the toiben," and I pointed to Erin.

Charlie smiled, shook his head and mouthed, "Nah. I'm good."

I made the introductions. Erin gave Charlie a very warm smile and extended her hand. He took it and said, "P-p-p-p-p." He stopped and took a breath. "Pleased to meet you."

Erin looked down, still smiling, and said, "Me too. You." Charlie still had hold of her hand and he squeezed it. She squeezed back. I didn't know about Charlie, but I was in love. Unfortunately, Erica saw me gawking at her sister.

Erica turned her attention to Charlie and went her sister one better, "I'm so excited to meet the famous Charlie Settler," and she gave him a hug. "Cutter, you never told me how handsome Charlie is." Charlie blushed.

Dinner went well, Charlie and Erin seemed to hit it off and Erica sat very close to me and kept putting her hand on my thigh. I was starting to think this prom might be monumental. I mean, like second-base monumental. When it came time for the check, I motioned for the waitress to come over and I asked her for it. She smiled, nodded at Charlie and said, "He already took care of it." Very smooth, Settler, very smooth.

As we walked out, Charlie whispered to me, "C-c-c-can you walk Erica home? I kinda told Erin I would give her a ride."

I stared at him. I knew, heck everyone knew, he had a thing for Regan, so it was surprising he seemed so interested in Erin. "Well?" he asked.

"Sure. You bet." I put on my best dad voice. "Don't keep her out too late.

And be a gentleman." He punched me on the shoulder, a little too hard I thought.

****

Charlie and Regan sat on the couch in Shawn's home studio. Shawn was deep in conversation with Beckett over her rendition of the drum solo she was going to do for the short set their group was playing for the prom. Shawn wanted her to play the solo harder and faster; she wanted to not work up a sweat when she was wearing her formal. It appeared they were not going to come to an agreement.

"D-d-d-did you hear I have a date for the prom?" Charlie asked Regan.

She smiled. "Yes, I did. Stone's cousin Erin, right? I heard she's really cute."

"She's okay." Long pause. "I-I-I-I w-w-wanted to ask you, but I figured you'd be going with Shawn." She nodded. Charlie looked at his feet. "I l-l-l-ove you, you know."

Now she looked at her feet as well. "I know. And I love you, Charlie. You're the best friend I ever had. And I never want to lose that."

"I just wanted you to know. I like Erin a lot and we m-m-m-may keep seeing each other." He paused again. "But she'll n-n-n-never be you." Regan put her head on his shoulder and squeezed his arm.

CHAPTER TWENTY-NINE

The prom was actually pretty neat—everyone all dressed up. Shawn delivered the limo as promised and, to keep it all in the family, so to speak, Stone had asked Beckett to go with him. He told her to go ahead and play the solo as hard and fast as she could, since he liked his girls sweaty. She punched him, but got an ovation when she outdid Keith Moon. And then threatened Stone with a whiff of her underarms.

The after-party was at Miller Time and as well chaperoned as it was, Shawn managed to get vodka past the guards by ferrying it in in some kind of water waist pack designed for long distance runners. He had told his folks he was buying the thing because he was going to get in shape by running that summer. He lied.

It was like two in the morning, we had gone through the vodka by sneaking it into our Cokes and we were all feeling pretty clever and grown up. We had claimed a couple of the bowling lanes and had a boy versus girl game going: me, Stone, Charlie and Shawn against Regan, Erica, Erin and Beckett. They were kicking our butts.

There was a huge crash behind us and we all looked up to see Bruce Creager, the kid called Chubbs, falling over a rack of bowling balls. Scott was standing over him, yelling at him to "get away and stay the fuck away." Chubbs was, as I mentioned before, one of Olsen's crew of misfits, but apparently he had fallen into disfavor with his overlord. The chaperones were on Scott immediately, pinning his arms behind him and propelling him to the door. Scott yelled over his shoulder, "Never talk to me again, you fucking loser!" The rest of Scott's crew dutifully followed him out the door.

Charlie had leapt to his feet and was next to Chubbs before Chubbs' ample belly had stopped jiggling from the impact with the rack. He helped Chubbs to his feet and guided him back to our seats and had him sit next to Erin. "Y-y-y-ou okay?" You could see tears in the guy's eyes, but he nodded his head.

"What happened?" asked Stone.

"I dunno," Chubbs told him.

"Why did he push you down? You musta done something."

"I din't do nuthin."

"What did you say to him?"

"Nuthin. I just said I thought you guys are pretty cool. That's all I said. Then he yelled at me, called me stupid and pushed me down."

Shawn laughed. "Well, yeah, I imagine your boy Olsen didn't like that much. He kinda doesn't cotton to us, for some reason." He then introduced Chubbs to the girls.

Erica told him, "Everyone knows any group that has Cutter in it can't be cool. Maybe that's why he said you were dumb." Everyone laughed, including Chubbs. Everyone but me.

Regan said, "Hey, Bruce, if you want to hang with us, that'd be great. You wanta bowl with us?"

"Yeah, I'm really good at bowling." Chubbs paused, then, "Thanks guys. Stupid Scott". Chubbs hung out with us the rest of the night. At five in the morning, the sky was lightening and we were released by our captors to pile into Shawn's limo to go to his house for breakfast. Chubbs followed us out and waved goodbye. Charlie looked at Shawn, who nodded his head, and yelled, "Hey, Chubbs, we're going to breakfast. You wanta go?"

Chubbs frowned. "I can't. I ain't got no money.

Shawn waved him over. "Don't need any. We're goin' to my house. Mom's makin' breakfast. Hop in. We'll get you home after." Big grin from Chubbs and he almost fell down waddling over to the limo.

For some reason, Chubbs sort of attached himself to Charlie. After breakfast, we hung out in the music studio, fooling around with the guitars and drums. Charlie showed Chubbs how to play a couple of chords and I swear to God, I've never seen a happier kid. Charlie even started calling him Bruce. By noon, everyone was rubbing their eyes and yawning, so Mr. Allen announced time for us to leave and the limo driver took us all home. Turned out Chubbs lived just a couple of blocks from Charlie. Chubbs went, in one night, from being part of Olsen's posse to being Charlie's entire posse. You can take the follower away from his leader, but you can't keep him from being a follower.

Stone and I ended up working together that summer as night stock boys at the Hy-Vee grocery store on Kimberly. It was about as perfect a summer before your senior year as a guy could have. We quickly fell into a routine. We worked from midnight to eight in the morning, Tuesday through Saturday. We'd leave work, damned near every day, drive through the McDonald's for breakfast and head to Duck Creek golf course where we'd get in a quick eighteen holes and go home to eat, sleep, eat and back to work. Repeat. All summer long.

I was still dating Erica, who remained permanently pissed that I had to work Friday and Saturday nights, which she considered the high holy nights for dating. But my charms and willingness to spend money on her meant that by midsummer, not only were we still dating, but I had actually gotten to second base. Where I remained stranded until my third year of college.

Stone continued his quest to date every girl in town before he graduated. And, if he was to be believed, he had not only gotten beyond second base, he had actually homered a couple of times. I did not believe him. For one thing, his golf game got much better. So I knew he had to be practicing. And he spent important date nights with me, being king of the pickle jars and lord of the cans of beans.

We didn't see much of the gang that summer. Shawn had shipped off to some fancy summer-long music internship run by the Chicago Symphony Orchestra. Berklee College of Music, which he was going to attend the next year, had strongly suggested he needed to spend more time on classical music, and his parents arranged (with the help of a sizable donation) for him to spend the summer in Chicago. He came home some weekends but spent them with Regan.

Regan was working as a daytime hostess at Ross' Restaurant and we saw her occasionally which is how we kept up with the news. She also spent time with Charlie since they both worked days.

Charlie had gotten a job at Deere as a drafting trainee, but it took the engineers he worked for not long to discover his talents and he was put on a design team working on alternative fuel tractors. He had hired Chubbs to run his lawn care business. Chubbs wasn't the sharpest pencil in the pack, in fact he was more like a broken-off crayon, and Charlie had spent the first three weeks of summer vacation nights and weekends showing Chubbs how to cut and trim every lawn. But the arrangement made both of them money. At least until the end of summer when Chubbs mowed down Mrs. Dodge's prize rose bushes. It cost Charlie several hundred dollars and a good client. It cost Chubbs his job. Chubbs never got over it. Once again, Chubbs was an outsider.

Charlie was still dating Erin so I saw him at Sunday events at the Denners. Mrs. Denner ("Oh, please, boys, call me Connie") was a stickler for Sunday family dinner so most Sundays, Charlie and I would meet at the 10:00 A.M. mass then head over to the Denners. He drove. He had finally finished the work on his 280Z and it was totally rad. He had spent more than a few bucks on a new paint job and interior leather, but he told me he could probably get at least ten grand for it.

Anyway, we'd tool on over to the girls' house and make nice with the family (there must have been about a dozen and a half of them), then eat, play with the little kids and afterwards take the girls to a movie or whatever suited their needs that day. As I said, I liked Erica, she was cute and funny and liked to make out, but there was something special about her sister. Erin had this way about her and she seemed to fit Charlie so well. I don't think I had ever seen him as relaxed as when he was with her. He smiled. He didn't stutter. And he was engaging. Heck, I wanted to date him.

It was a great summer. The last of the great summers. I have always believed life is really just an ongoing struggle to achieve homeostasis, balance in how you interact with the natural world, with other beings and with your own body and mind. Life's greatest joys, however, lie in anticipation. The first ball teed up on the first tee—it may be the best round of your life; the opening credits of a movie—it may be the best movie you ever saw; looking at the bridge hand dealt to you; it may be a lay down grand slam; the meal at a good restaurant—it may be the best food you have ever eaten. The moment between when you know you are going to kiss her and the moment you do. The opening paragraph of a new Robin Yocum book. You get it. There are, or should be, thousands of those moments in a life. From the big ones like weddings, to the smallest of them, like being handed a warm chocolate chip cookie just out of the oven.

That summer, the summer of 1991, was like that. Ten weeks of anticipation of the best things ever to come.

Then we had our senior year.

CHAPTER THIRTY

My dad shook me awake. "What?" I grumped. "What time is it?" It was dark out and very cold, like in colder than a well digger's ass in January cold. Two thirty in the morning, November 4, 1991. Turned out it was twelve degrees.

"Get up. Get dressed. We have to leave in two minutes, so move it." He used his dad voice. Not an angry one, but the one that you knew was serious. Very serious.

"What's wrong?" I was almost afraid to ask.

"We'll talk about it in the car. Move it, Winston."

I pulled on jeans and a hoodie and was waiting in the car when Dad climbed in. Mom had been in the kitchen brewing coffee so I knew there was nothing wrong with her or the family. "Okay, so what's wrong? Where are we going?"

"We're going to the sheriff's office. Charlie's been arrested."

"What the fuck?" It was out of my mouth before I could check it. Old Henry gave me the evil eye but didn't say anything. "Sorry. I mean, what happened? Why was he arrested? Why are we going there?" Charlie? Arrested? It made no sense. For a few seconds, I realized I was dreaming and I smiled. Only I wasn't.

"Apparently he stole a car. They couldn't reach his folks, so he gave them our number. We're picking him up and taking him to our house. Since he's a juvenile, they didn't want to put him in lock up." He paused. "That's all I know. We'll find out more when we get there. I'm sure it's just a big mix up. I hope." He drove the rest of the ten minutes downtown in silence.

When we got there, I sat in the waiting room while Dad went back to talk to the deputy. He was gone about twenty minutes and when he came out,

Charlie was walking next to him. I started to say something and Charlie frowned at me and shook his head, "no." We rode home, Charlie in the back seat, me in the front looking straight ahead. Mom met us at the door and grabbed Charlie and hugged him so hard I thought his eyes might pop out. We had coffee and Mom had made biscuits. It was weird but I was famished. Mom offered to make scrambled eggs and Charlie and I both jumped on the offer. After we ate, he told us what had happened.

****

The school year started just as we had envisioned. We were cocks of the walk, big cheeses, supreme commanders of all we surveyed. We were, wait for it, Seniors. We spent the first couple of weeks lording it over all the lesser beings, but most of all, the lowly freshmen. While initiation had been banned, at least officially, we found ways of making the ninth graders' lives a living hell. If they sat down in the lunch room or in the gym, we told them they were in our seats. We took stuff off their lunch plates. We jimmied the lockers so they couldn't get the doors open. Sometimes, they got accidently bumped in the hall and would drop what they were carrying. Backpacks got opened and rifled through, though we were careful not to take anything. It was grand, at least for a few weeks, until they caught on and started pushing back… just as we had when we endured the "welcome to high school".

We spent a lot of time on college applications. We'd all taken the SATs in the spring (And Stone took it again in the summer, on account of his crappy score) and Father Bouvier, the guidance counselor, made us pick at least three colleges to apply to. We all knew where we were going, we were certain of it, but he said we had to have back-ups, you know, just like the less fortunate among us who wouldn't get into a good school. I was going to the University of Chicago but also applied to Northwestern and Loyola to make Bouvier happy.

Stone didn't apply to any. He was waiting to see who offered him the best basketball scholarship. He'd had nibbles from Drake and Northern Illinois, but he was holding out for Indiana or, as an also ran, Notre Dame. Father urged him to maybe apply, you know, just as a safety net, somewhere. Stone just grinned. Shawn and Charlie were set. In fact, Dr. Jakubs from Purdue came to St. Al for a big signing event for Charlie's scholarship. His mom and brother Jimmie came for it and they all got their picture in the Quad City Times. It was pretty neat.

Regan applied to Penn and Temple and, I suppose, to be close to Shawn, Boston College. Lynne only applied to in-state schools. She said she wanted to be closer to home. Well, to each his own, I guess. I couldn't wait to get away from Davenport, from Iowa, from hogs and farmland and small town thinking. Though, of course, when the Quad Cities get their hooks into you, you never really escape.

Other than at school, we didn't see much of each other. Charlie had a couple of part-time jobs and was trying to save money for school. He still had Chubbs working for him and had taken the kid under his wing, teaching him about motors and cars and equipment. He told me it was an uphill job, but that Chubbs was okay and he thought he owed it to him, since other people had helped him the same way. Stone was hard at work on basketball. Shawn spent a lot of time with his guitar (I think his summer with the Chicago Symphony Orchestra convinced him he may still have a lot to learn) and Regan was working as well. Lynne was into cheerleading and her new Bettendorf boyfriend. And I was still making out with Erica.

****

"Hey, uh, Charlie, it's Bruce. I need your help."

"G-g-g-geez, Chubbs, it's almost eleven. I gotta be at work before school tomorrow. Can't it wait?"

"No, man. I'm in real trouble and you're the only one who can help. You just gotta come."

Charlie looked at his aunt, who had answered the phone, and mouthed, "Sorry," and then asked Chubbs, "Where are you?" His aunt smiled at him and returned to her bedroom.

"I'm at home. You gotta come help me."

"What's wrong?"

"Come over and I'll tell ya."

"Damnit." Charlie paused and shook his head slowly. "Alright. I'll be there in fifteen minutes. B-b-b-but you'll owe me one." He stepped outside, realized how cold it was and went back in to get his parka. He climbed in the 280Z and five minutes later pulled up in front of Chubbs' house. Chubbs was sitting on the top step of the porch. As soon as the car rolled to a stop, Chubbs was in the passenger door.

"Thanks, man. I'm gonna be in big trouble if you don't help me."

"Wh-wh-wh-what's wrong?"

"Man, I borrowed my uncle's car without telling him and I was up at the McDonald's on Kimberly and I got somepin' to eat and then I was driving down Eastern and I spilled my coffee and I hadda pull over to clean it up and I stopped the car and I got out to clean it up on accounta my uncle would kill me if I got something on the seat of his special car and somehow I

175

dropped the key and I couldn't find it and so I walked home and called you and you just gotta help me get his car back to his house before he gets up or I'll be in big trouble and my folks'll kill me…" He stopped talking because he was out of breath and started making crying sounds.

"What can I do? I don't have a key or know how to make one. Do you want me to help you look for it?'

"I dunno. It's an old car and I thought maybe you would know how to start it without a key. I can get another key made tomorrow while he's at work. Man, you gotta help me."

"What kind of car?"

"I dunno. Some old Chevy, like thirty years old or somepin'. My uncle, he like restored it. Like you did with this car. It's like this big deal or somepin'."

Charlie stared out through the windshield. "Alright. Let's go look at it."

Chubbs guided him up Eastern and had him turn on 35th. Right after 35th turned into Adams, Chubbs pointed at a car parked by the side of the street. "That's it." Charlie pulled up behind the car and thought, "Sure ain't much of a restoration. 1960 Chevy Impala. Nice car." Chubbs got out and opened the driver side door to the Chevy.

"Can you start it?"

"Doncha think we should look for the key?"

"I did. I tell ya it ain't here. Please, Charlie, can't you wire it or somepin'?"

Charlie walked around the car with a flashlight he kept in his glove compartment and looked for anything metallic on the ground. Nothing. Finally he bent down to look beneath the steering wheel. He'd actually done this before—something the guys in auto shop taught him. He grabbed a couple of wires, used his fingernail to scratch the insulation off and touched them together. The motor coughed a couple of times and came alive. He stood up and put his gloves back on. "There you go. Don't turn it off."

Chubbs looked confused. "Ain't you gonna drive it for me? What if it cuts off? I can't start it."

"Just go straight back to your uncle's. I'll follow you."

"Please, Charlie. You drive it there and I'll pick you up in your car. Please."

"Where's your uncle live?"

"Out offa Locust. Just past the freeway. First house after 110th. Ya can't miss it. Brick house. I'll be right behind you. Park it and turn it off and lock the door when you get out."

Charlie slid behind the wheel and slowly drove out to Eastern, down it and right on Locust, heading west out of town. He kept the lights of the 280Z in his rearview mirror, but at Division Street, Chubbs didn't make the light, so he slowed, hoping the Z car would catch up. Right after he passed over the freeway, the rearview mirror lit up with flashing red lights. He pulled over at the bottom of the westbound exit. Rolled down his window and waited, hoping Chubbs would show up quickly.

"Keep your hands where I can see them and step out of the car." The Scott County deputy sounded very serious. A second deputy stood behind him with his hand on his revolver. Charlie did as he was told. As soon as he was out of the car, the deputy spun him around. "Hands on the roof of the vehicle, spread your legs and don't move a muscle."

"Wh-wh-wh-wh-wh," Charlie stuttered and stopped. He tried again, "Why did you stop m-m-m-me?"

"This car was reported stolen. We're placing you under arrest. Put your hands behind your back." Charlie complied and they handcuffed him. As they turned him around to march him to the patrol car, a car slowed to pass them and its window came down. Scott Olsen was grinning at him. Scott gave him the finger and waved, mouthing, "Fuck you." In the back seat behind Scott sat Chubbs also grinning. The car sped off .

CHAPTER THIRTY-ONE

Charlie told us what had happened. The more he talked, the madder I got. Those assholes. And it sounded like it had been a set up from the very beginning. Though I couldn't fathom Bruce Creager being smart enough to figure or stick with a plan like that. Of course, it had been Olsen's plan and Chubbs was just the stooge.

After Charlie finished his story, I said, "Well, that just isn't fair. I'm sure when we tell people what happened, they'll let Charlie go, right?"

My dad shook his head. "No, Cutter, that's not how it works. For one thing, no matter what the extenuating circumstances are, Charlie did in fact hotwire and drive the car. And what if Bruce denies it? How would he prove it?" He stopped and thought for a minute. "Perhaps if a good attorney got Bruce on the witness stand in a trial, he could get him to confess, but attorneys cost a lot and there is no guarantee that would change the outcome. What would the argument be? 'Your Honor, my client was too dumb to know he was being tricked and should be let off.' It doesn't change the facts."

Charlie asked, "How much does a lawyer cost?"

"I don't know in this case, but my coworker's daughter got arrested for speeding and underage drinking and it cost the woman $5,000 just to have her daughter plead guilty. And that was just a misdemeanor. Charlie's crime is a felony. The court will provide a public defender for free, but they will want to plead out the case."

"What do you think Charlie should do?"

"We should think about it. Charlie has a court appearance the day after tomorrow so we have some time. You guys need to get to sleep." He turned to Charlie. "Can you skip school in the morning?"

"I have work before that I can't miss. And I don't know where my car is."

"It was on the street where the stolen car was. And it was impounded. Your lawyer will have to ask the court to return it so you can get to work and school. I'll take you to work and school in the morning. Get a couple hours of sleep. And try not to worry. We'll get this sorted out. You should call your mom tomorrow as well."

By the time I got to school, the rumors were all over the place. Charlie was in jail. Charlie had beaten some kid up. The cops had beaten Charlie and he was in the hospital. He had tried to sell a stolen car to an undercover cop. He was involved with drugs. He had gotten his girlfriend pregnant and was skipping town. My personal favorite was that Stone and I were arrested with him. Olsen and his thugs had made sure everyone heard all the stories.

When Charlie got there, he was immediately whisked to Principal Morgan's office and then escorted out of the building.

At lunch our crew sat together trying to figure out what was going on. We were all pretty shell shocked. Olsen came over to our table, Chubbs, big Johnny Cooper and John Peterson, the kid we called Pimps, all trailing behind. Scott grinned and said, loud enough for the entire cafeteria to hear, "Hey, I heard your friend Settler got arrested for car theft. Bad news. Just the kind of loser you guys would hang with." He would have gone on, but Alan Johnson rose to his full six foot ten height and offered to punch him again.

Scott backed away and as he was leaving, yelled over his shoulder, "You bunch of pathetic losers. I hope he rots in jail."

Lynne said something to Regan and they both started crying. We didn't know what to do. Somebody suggested we pool our money to hire him a lawyer until I told them how much that would be. I told them what Charlie had told us. We made a pact we would all stick with him, no matter what.

The next day Charlie appeared in court. My dad took him and his mom had shown up as well. There was a lot of legaling and Charlie was given a bond of $500 which his mother paid. When the judge ruled Charlie could not leave Scott County, Charlie turned pale and whispered to his lawyer, who asked to speak with Charlie's mother. Mrs. Settler's best friend, Charlie's "aunt," had told Charlie he had to leave her house. My dad overheard and volunteered to host him. The judge agreed so Charlie moved in with us, at least until the trial.

The really bad news was the newspaper. Normally such an incident would garner no more than one line in the police blotter report. But because the *QC Times* had made such a big deal out of Charlie's scholarship, they decided to run a whole story about it, under the headline "Young Scholar Arrested".

"Cutter, I , uh," Erica's voice trailed off.

"Yeah?" I answered into the phone.

"We have to talk." Never a good thing, I had already learned. "We have to talk" is code for "bye-bye, Cutter". "Could you please meet me at Lagomarcino's?"

"It's a little cold for ice cream, doncha think?"

Her voice went from warm to cold. "Fine. You pick a place. But we have to talk."

I met her at Lagomarcino's. We had hot chocolate. She had obviously been crying. I put on the old debonair, nonchalant Cutter voice. "So, what's up, Buttercup?" Bad choice.

"Please, Cutter." Her eyes welled up. I tried a different tactic. I took hold of her hand and she squeezed tightly. "We can't see each other anymore. I mean, we can't date anymore."

Duh. That was pretty obvious. "Why? What did I do?"

"Nothing. It's not you, it's (Man, this was right out of every breakup you've ever heard about. 'It's not you, it's me…') my father. He says I can't go with you anymore."

"Your father?" I mean, I knew old man Denner didn't like me much. Nor Charlie. He thought his little princesses should be dating football captains and bankers' sons, not us riffraff from the wrong side of the tracks. Well, screw him. "What's he upset about?"

"After he heard about Charlie getting arrested, he told Erin she couldn't see him anymore, and she had a fit and said it wasn't fair and that if she couldn't see Charlie, then I shouldn't be able to see you 'cause you guys are friends and he found out Charlie is living with you and told me I can't see you and I hate him and I hate Erin and Charlie and it's just not fair and I'm so, so sorry, Cutter. I really like you and…" at this point she was full on crying and all I could do was hold her hand tighter.

Finally, the crying turned to sniffles and I said, "Don't worry, this will all be over soon. The truth will come out and everyone will see Charlie is not to blame here. And things will get back to normal." Yeah, right. I couldn't have been more wrong. We hugged and kissed outside the restaurant. It was the last time I ever kissed her. I was gonna miss that.

When I got home, Charlie told me Erin had called him and they had broken up. I told him about Erica. "I'm s-s-s-sorry I f-f-f-fucked things up. I really was j-j-just trying to help the guy."

"Ah, don't worry about it. It's not like Erica and I were gonna get married or anything. Besides, someday when we're rich and famous, they'll be sorry. And their old man can kiss our butts."

Things returned to semi-normal at school. Principal Morgan held an assembly and reminded everyone that "in our country, everyone is presumed innocent until proven guilty," which brought hoots from Olsen and his minions, all of whom earned in-school suspensions. Which they blamed on Charlie, of course. It sort of felt like we were on the verge of all-out war.

Our crew stayed pretty low key. The Denner girls were gone and Stone spent all his time on the court or with his teammates. He seemed distant, probably trying to remain neutral but not screw up his local hero status. Shawn also seemed to push Charlie away, not overtly, but in lots of little ways. It was like Charlie had some disease or something. Only Regan stayed tight with him.

The holidays came and went. The basketball team won a big regional tournament and shortly thereafter, Alan, all six foot ten of him, and Stone were both offered scholarships to Iowa. I was waitlisted by U of Chicago. And, at the end of January, was Charlie's trial.

CHAPTER THIRTY-TWO

Three days before his trial, Charlie sat in the small public defender's office in an even smaller little cubicle, one obviously reserved for the newest of the attorneys who worked there. He appeared calm on the outside, but inside he was knotted with fear. He stared quietly at the grease embedded in his knuckles.

"Hello. Mr. Settler?" The young woman, who looked to Charlie to be even younger than he was, stood in the doorway. She was barely five feet tall, slender, cute and wore her brunette hair in a side ponytail, making her look like she was a seventh grader.

"Yes?" Charlie answered.

The woman squeezed into the office and behind her desk. She remained standing and offered her hand to Charlie. He wiped his hand on his pants and shook hers. "My name is Mrs. Sparks. I'm your court appointed attorney." She sat. She was not what Charlie was expecting. He was hoping for an Arnie Becker from *LA Law*; he would have settled for a Christine Sullivan from *Night Court*. Like all of us, everything he knew about lawyers came from television.

"Yes, ma'am. N-n-n-nice to meet you."

Mrs. Sparks sorted through a stack of papers on her desk and pulled out a thin file. She read the three pages of reports in the file then looked up. "Car theft?" she said, a bit of disbelief in her voice.

"I can explain."

"Tell me your side of the story." Charlie recounted the events of the incident. She made notes as he talked.

After he finished, she asked, "So what made you believe the car actually belonged to your friend's uncle?"

Charlie shook his head. "I dunno. I thought he was a friend. You know, a good guy."

"M-m-m-m."

"D-d-do you think that will matter at the trial?"

"Mr. Settler, Charles, you're a juvenile. I don't think there should be a trial. It's a first offense, the court's pre-trial review indicates you are a good student and employed, and I see you have a scholarship to college. I believe your best option is to plead 'guilty' and I think we can get the sentence reduced to a fine and probation and maybe some community service. Would you like me to pursue that with the district attorney's office?"

Charlie asked, "How much would the fine be?"

"I don't know for sure," she shuffled the papers in her hand. "Maybe $1,000."

"That's a lot. I-I-I-I only have a couple thousand saved up for school." He stared at his hands again.

"Your decision. I should tell you. I've never actually been to trial. But I'll do my best for you." She smiled.

"Okay. Talk to the other lawyer." Charlie looked defeated. He had believed there might be a miracle cure but realized that was just a dream. He promised himself to pay back Scottt Olsen and that weasel Chubbs Creager.

"Will your parents be at the court for your hearing?"

"Maybe my mom. Not my stepdad." He paused. "Maybe Mr. Williams, the family I live with now."

"Great. May I talk with them before the hearing?" Charlie gave her their phone numbers.

****

Three days later we sat in the courtroom. Had it not been for the reason we were there, it would have been pretty exciting. Dad, Mom and I sat at the back. Charlie's lawyer had asked Dad to speak on Charlie's behalf and Dad told her he would be happy to. He was nervous. He kept fidgeting with his tie and drumming his fingers on his leg.

The judge looked like he was a thousand years old, lots of gray hair and wrinkles. He wore his glasses out on the end of his nose and wheezed when he talked. After the lawyers met in front of his bench and they talked for a few minutes, he asked Charlie to stand. Mrs. Sparks stood next to him, over a foot shorter. Charlie was right. She looked like a seventh grader.

"Mr. Settler, I understand you have agreed to plead guilty to grand theft auto. Am I correct?"

"Yessir," Charlie responded, his voice very low.

"Speak up, Son," the judge ordered.

Much louder this time. "Y-y-y-yessir."

"Do you have anything else you would like to say?" Charlie looked at Mrs. Sparks and she shook her head.

"N-n-n-no sir."

"Therefore, the Court accepts your plea of guilty and sentences you to probation until you reach your eighteenth birthday." You could see Charlie's shoulders relax and I just knew he was smiling. The judge continued, "And a fine of $12,500. Should you not be able to pay said fine, you will be remanded to the custody of the Iowa Juvenile Detention Center until your eighteenth birthday. So ordered. Case dismissed. Next case." And he rapped his gavel once on the bench.

"Th-th-th-th-that's not fair," Charlie practically yelled at the judge.

The judge rapped the gavel again, this time harder, and said, "Careful, Son, you don't want to make it worse."

As they walked out, Charlie said to his lawyer, "I-I-I-I-I thought you said it would only be $1,000. I don't have $12,000. They're going to put me in jail. This is not fair. I'm gonna kill Olsen and Chubbs and all the rest of 'em. What am I going to do?"

Mrs. Sparks told him, "Charlie, the Court knows you have a car worth a lot of money and I told them you would sell it as part of the settlement plea."

"Y-y-y-you had no right to do that. It's my car. I'm not gonna sell it."

By this time, they had reached our seats and my dad was on his feet, putting his hand on Charlie's shoulder. Charlie jerked away from him, but Dad grabbed his shoulder again, harder this time and said, very softly, "Charlie, we'll figure this out. This is no time to lose your temper." Charlie looked at him and then at me. He made a face I had never seen on him before. Determined, angry and mean. I actually backed away from him.

Charlie did not speak on the ride home. He went straight up to his bedroom and closed the door. When Mom called for everyone to come to supper, he did not respond. She knocked on his door and he told her to go away. She left a plate outside his door and when I went up to bed, I saw the plate was gone. Dad told us we should just give him some time.

The next morning when I got up, he was already gone. He got to school and went to classes and spoke to no one, not even me or Shawn or anyone in the group. He spent the day watching the floor or staring out the window. Before the last class of the day, Lynne approached him in the hall and he asked, very politely, that she not talk to him. She tried again and he snapped at her. We all left him alone. I assumed he would come out of it.

Three days later, he asked my dad to pick him up at Lujack's car dealership at ten that morning. Lujack's had agreed to buy his car for $9000. Dad took him to the bank where he took all the money from his savings account, $3,000, and Dad lent him the other $500 to pay his fine. They went to the courthouse and Charlie gave them a cashier's check for the whole amount. Dad said Charlie had cried when he left the car dealership.

CHAPTER THIRTY-THREE

"Hello?"

"Charlie, it's Regan."

"Hi." Pause. "Wh-wh-what do you want?"

"I want you to quit acting like an asshole."

By the end of March, Charlie had completely withdrawn from the world. He went to work, both before and after school; at home he ate with us; he did his chores. But he didn't talk to anyone except for curt, stuttered answers when directly addressed. The only person he even smiled at was my mom. She told us we should just give him some space. Father Bouvier, the guidance counselor, hauled him into his office and tried to walk him through his anger but nothing changed. He would have nothing to do with our group or anyone in it.

"Okay," was his complete answer to Regan.

"Charlie, come have dinner with me at the Village Inn, please."

"Will Shawn or anyone else be there?"

"No, just you and me."

"When?"

"I'll be there in fifteen minutes."

"Alright." Charlie put on a clean shirt and went out to the truck he was driving, the old one he had gotten from a farm. He'd used the first $400 he had earned after the trial to buy it, after Dad told him not to worry about paying him back the loan for the fine. Dad had told him when he was a rich engineer he could pay him back.

Charlie arrived just as Regan was getting to the front door of the restaurant. She waited for him and he let her hug him before they went inside. There was no conversation until they had ordered.

"Charlie, you have to quit acting like this."

"Acting like what?"

"You know. We miss you. I miss you. We need our friend back." He frowned. "C'mon Charlie. You're better than this."

"They took everything from me. All my life they've been taking from me and I-I-I-I-I got nothing left to give."

"That's a load of crap. You've got friends, you've got a place to live with folks who care for you and, Charlie, you've got a great future. A scholarship to go to a good school, you're healthy and some place out there is a girl who will deserve you." Tears came into her eyes.

His face softened. He put his hand on the table and she covered it with her hand. They sat that way until the food arrived.

"Friday night we're going to hang out in the music room at Shawn's. You should come. Everyone's gonna be there."

"I dunno. Maybe."

"For me?"

"Okay. Maybe you could invite Chubbs so I can stick a guitar up his ass." Charlie finally smiled.

****

Friday night, the first Friday in April, the weather was starting to warm some and it felt like spring might actually show up sometime. We'd been invited to hang out at Shawn's for a little celebration. The basketball team had made it to the state semi-finals where they had lost because both Alan and Stone had somehow managed to foul out. So we were celebrating their loss and their return to civilian life. Oh, and my birthday, which had happened during the tournament.

When I went downstairs to leave for Shawn's, Charlie was sitting in the living room. It was the first time I'd seen him in something other than the old clothes he wore to work and school.

"M-m-mind if I ride with you?" he asked. I was shocked. It was like the first thing he had said to me in weeks. And he was going to hang out with us.

"That'd be great. What's in the bag?"

"Olsen's head," and he laughed. "It's your birthday present."

Everyone was a little wary of Charlie when we first arrived. Lynne sat in a corner and refused to even acknowledge his presence. It didn't take Charlie long to notice. He walked over to her, grabbed her hands and pulled her up so they were nose to nose. "Red, I'm sorry I've been such a shit," and before she could respond, he took her face in his hands and kissed her. Swear to God, the girl almost swooned.

But it broke the ice and we were pretty much back to where we had been six months before. We had sodas, some spiked with a little vodka Shawn had filched from the liquor cabinet, and we chatted and made fun of each other and talked about school and college and the misery that had been the state basketball tournament.

The pizza arrived, we chowed down and then Mrs. Allen brought in a birthday cake. Well, half of it was a birthday cake. The other half was decorated with a little basketball hoop and ball. The members of Blake's Tyger grabbed their instruments and started playing and singing. "Happy birthday to you, happy birthday to you. Happy birthday, dear Cutter, happy birthday to you." Before I could react, they started another round of the same tune. "Crappy tournament loss for you, crappy tournament loss for you. Crappy tournament loss, Stone and Alan, better luck at the U." Stone looked a little miffed, but everyone else roared with laughter. It was so good to be back to normal.

Charlie was back to being Charlie. The only time I saw any anger was when he would see Olsen or Chubbs. He told me on more than one occasion, he was gonna make them pay. When Regan heard him say it, she grabbed his arm and dug her fingernails into his bicep until he winced. "Charles Settler, I am gonna tell you something and I want you to repeat it and I want you to tell me you understand what it means. Got it?" He nodded. "'Living well is the best revenge.' I read that once in an article about Fitzgerald. Do you understand what I'm telling you?"

Charlie would have agreed to anything to stop the nails in his arms, but he told her, "I get it. I should give up being p-p-p-pissed at them and leave them alone." She nodded, smiled and let his arm go. He rubbed it.

"Repeat it."

"Living well is the best revenge."

"Good. Now go do it."

The first week in May, Charlie got home from his after school job just in time for dinner. While we were eating, Mom said, "Oh, Charlie, I forgot. You got a letter from Purdue. It's on the coffee table in the living room." After dinner he and I cleaned up the dishes and I told him I'd finish washing them. He went into the living room.

Two minutes later I heard him stomp upstairs and two minutes after that, stomp down the stairs and slam the door on the way out. His old truck backfired as he revved the motor and then sped away. Dad stuck his head in the kitchen and asked, "What was that all about?" I shrugged my shoulders.

Mom called out from the living room, "Henry, you better come look at this." We went into the living room and she handed Dad the letter from Purdue.

Dear Mr. Settler:

We regret to inform you that in accordance with our rules and regulations governing student behavior, we are herewith withdrawing our offer of an academic scholarship. Rule 32-146.1 states, "Any student convicted of a felony is automatically ineligible to receive student assistance of any kind, including scholarships, loans and other support. Any student forfeiting his or her support may appeal the decision and ask for reinstatement after a period of not less than twenty-four (24) months."

We are sure you can appreciate the need for such a rule at a public university which receives state support. This ruling does not affect your acceptance to our program and we sincerely hope you will choose to join us in the fall.

Sincerely,

John F. Jakubs

John F. Jakubs, PhD
Dean, College of Engineering

Christ in a handbasket.

CHAPTER THIRTY-FOUR

Charlie didn't come home that night. He wasn't in school the next day. He didn't show up for either his morning office cleaning job nor his after school job at the engineering firm. I checked with everyone in the group, starting with Shawn and Regan 'cause those were his best two friends. Shawn said not to worry that Charlie would show up when he got over being mad. Regan flipped out. She wanted to call the sheriff's office and have him classified as a missing person. We talked her out of that.

My mom called Charlie's mom to see if they had heard from him. They hadn't and both agreed to call the other if he turned up. Dad called the "aunt" he had lived with most of his time in Davenport. The woman screamed at him, "No, I haven't heard from him and he better not show up here or I'll call the cops. That boy is no good, stealing cars and who knows what else." Dad let her rant, then hung up without saying a word.

The office he cleaned for called mom and said to tell Charlie, "Please come back to work. You're the best worker we've ever had and we know you have been unfairly treated, so we'll hold your job for you as long as you need us to. We've hired a temp firm until you get back." It made my mom cry.

Two days later Mrs. Settler called and said Charlie was with them and okay. He asked her to apologize to us and said we shouldn't worry. My mom cried again.

****

Charlie knocked on the door of the doublewide on the outskirts of Ottumwa. His sister, half-sister, Carol, answered the door. She just stood and stared at Charlie for a full minute, then squealed and grabbed him. "Oh,

Charlie," she said without lessening her hold on him, "We have all been so worried about you. Where have you been?" and before he could answer, "Never mind. I'm just so happy you're okay and you're here."

Charlie hadn't seen her in a couple of years and was amazed at the change in her. She was no longer the skinny, freckle-faced kid he remembered. She was now sixteen and still had the freckles but was as pretty as his mom had been when she was that age. "Hey, k-k-k-kid. How's it goin'?"

"Mom," Carol yelled to the back of the house. "Charlie's here and he's okay." By the time Mrs. Settler reached the living room, tears were rolling down her face. She hugged him and led him to the kitchen where she forced him to sit while she made him a huge lunch. He hadn't realized it, but he had not eaten anything for a couple of days, except some candy bars and sodas, and was famished. He scarfed down two sandwiches and chips and was starting on a piece of pie before he told them what had happened with his scholarship. They already knew but let him talk it through.

"So what are you gonna to do now?" Carol asked.

"I don't know. I just don't know." He paused. "Getting even with Olsen and Chubbs would be a good place to start."

"Who're they?" Carol asked.

"The guys who set me up to get arrested. This is all their fault."

Mrs. Settler frowned and shook her head. "No, Charlie, don't even think about that. That'll lead nowhere. You should figure out how you can go to college and concentrate on that."

"R-r-really, Mom? You guys gonna pay for it? Great. Just write me a check and I'll be on my way to Purdue." He sounded meaner than he had meant to. His mom started crying again. "Sorry, Mom. I didn't mean that. I can't go. There is no money. Maybe I'll get a job and save and be able to go in a couple of years." He stopped. "Why did this have to happen?"

The three of them sat quietly for several minutes and Charlie started yawning. "I haven't slept much in the last couple of days. W-w-would it be alright if I take a nap?" He found his way to a back bedroom and was asleep before he could take off his shoes. He awoke four hours later when his stepfather started yelling at his mom.

"What the hell is that kid doing here? I don't want him in my house. Not now. Not ever. Kid's a loser. He was a bastard when he was born and he's still a bastard." Charlie heard his mom respond but could not hear what she said. The old man again, "He can stay the night, but I want him out of here in the morning." Charlie rubbed the sleep out of his eyes and went out to the living room, just in time to see Mr. Settler push his mom down on the floor.

Charlie launched himself at the old man, both of them falling to the floor next to a wide-eyed Mrs. Settler. Charlie was six two, lean, with arms made muscular by years of hard work. His stepdad was maybe five eight with a paunchy belly and no muscle at all. It was no match. Charlie did not see the old man for what he was. He saw him for what he had been when Charlie was a kid. It was that younger, vile man he started hitting. He sat on the old man's chest and beat his face with both fists until his face was red with blood and his front teeth knocked out. Only then were his mother and sister able to pull him off.

Carol pushed her brother away from the old man. Mrs. Settle tended to her husband with a cold wash cloth. The old man sputtered and then yelled, "Call the cops, I want that asshole put in jail forever. Fuckin' little bastard." He spit blood all over his wife's shirt.

Carol grabbed Charlie by the front of his shirt and pushed him towards the door, whispering, "Charlie, you gotta get out of here. He'll have you arrested for sure. You gotta go now." Tears, lots of tears. "I love you. Go." And she shoved him out the door. Charlie got in his truck and drove off.

****

Four days later Charlie showed up at our house. When Mom answered the door, he asked her to come out onto the porch. "Mrs. Williams, I am s-s-s-so sorry for all the problems I've caused. If you s-s-s-say 'no', that's okay, but I would like to finish school and I have no place else to stay. I promise I won't cause any more problems." My mom put a finger to his lips, smiled and then guided him into the house.

When Stone and I got to my house after school, Charlie was there on the phone trying to get his after school job back. The engineering firm reluctantly agreed, though two days later when they found out he was not going to college, they fired him. The morning office cleaning job was glad to have him back.

Stone called Shawn and he came over, Regan in tow. Everyone told him how sorry they were about the scholarship thing and tried to cheer him up. He seemed, I don't know, just not there in a way, his voice was flat, his face passive, his smile forced. Like he was half asleep or in a trance.

"So," Shawn asked, "where did you go?"

"I dunno. Around."

"Around?"

Charlie hesitated. "I went to see my family. Up to see my grandpa. He lives in Cedar County. Went back to where I lived in DeWitt. You remember,

Cutter, out in the sticks. That old house has fallen down in places. Wh-wh-wh-what a shithole that was." His voice trailed off.

The next day, he went to work, then back to school and spent the day convincing his teachers to let him make up the work so he could graduate. His few friends all were nice enough to him, though everyone seemed to be cautious and gave him lots of space. He didn't seem to notice.

CHAPTER THIRTY-FIVE

After he retrieved the weapons from the lockbox in the back of the beat up old truck, he sat back down behind the wheel, fingering the assault rifle, watching kids hustling to first period class. He'd let them get settled, get involved with whatever was going on in class. When he'd gotten back in the truck, he'd taken the six shooter out of his waistband and laid it on the seat beside him. The rifle lay across his lap and he picked up the pistol. Cowboys and Indians. Yee-ha.

He knew exactly where he was going. Chemistry class. In the basement, in the science lab which always smelled of formaldehyde and acid. That's where Olsen would be and that was who he wanted to start with. If he only got one, that would be the one to get. He also wanted that fat ass Chubbs because he had replaced him as Olsen's number one guy. Chubbs would be in shop. Or detention. And shop was on the way back to his truck. He still had the thought he could escape, though he had made no plan on where to escape to. If others got in the way or tried to stop him, so be it. They'd get wasted.

He couldn't help that he had such bad acne. The doc said he would grow out of it, but that sure didn't help now. He hated when they called him "Pimps." Why couldn't they use his nickname from grade school. Petey hadn't been the best, but it was a lot better than Pimps. Or just use his real name, John Peterson.

Scott Olsen. When Scott let him hang around, it was the first time he was part of something. Other kids started giving him some respect. Nobody fucked with Olsen. Or Olsen's guys. Nobody but that goody two shoes, Charlie Settler. John would have been glad to help bring Settler down, but no, Olsen wanted Chubbs to do it and now Chubbs was the big guy in the outfit. Olsen still let him hang around but treated him like dirt. These guys were gonna pay. They were all gonna pay. Maybe even Settler and those turds he hung out with. All of 'em.

The campus had quieted. John opened the truck door and slid out, holding the rifle along his left leg. He reached in to take the keys, then thought that he should leave them in for a quick getaway. He grabbed the pistol and slid it into his waistband. The rifle felt heavier than he remembered. He kept it tucked next to his leg so if anyone saw him, they wouldn't see the rifle, at least not in time. He headed for the door.

Because Charlie had had to stay to meet with the office manager to do the paperwork for his reinstatement, he got to school about fifteen minutes late. He coasted into a parking space back by the ball diamond and grabbed his backpack. As he opened the door, he noticed a kid get out of another pickup truck about forty yards in front of him. The kid, he couldn't make out who it was, reached back into his truck and then straightened up. Charlie finally recognized Pimps, who was holding something against his leg.

It took a few seconds for the image to come together in Charlie's mind. It was a rifle, Pimps was carrying an automatic rifle. Moving towards the school. What was going on? It could hardly be show and tell. It took another ten seconds for the meaning to finally register. Oh shit. Oh shit. Oh, my God.

Charlie's instincts took over. He started moving, as fast as he could, to stop Pimps. The only way to do that and lessen the chance of either of them getting hurt by that rifle was to tackle him, low, down by the knees, and hope he couldn't get the rifle raised to fire. Charlie covered the forty or so yards in about six seconds and was within five yards before Pimps heard him coming. Pimps started to turn, just as Charlie left his feet for the tackle. He had turned enough so when Charlie hit him, it was in the side of his right knee. His tibia snapped like a wishbone.

Pimps had started to raise the rifle, but it was only halfway up and the safety still on when the searing pain hit. He sprawled, Charlie first on top of him and then rolling off. The rifle skidded ten feet in front of him on the pavement. Charlie was up and moving toward the weapon and Pimps was screaming in pain.

"What the fuck, Pimps?" Charlie grabbed the gun and stood up. Pimps tried to stand, couldn't and fell back down. He reached into his waistband and pulled out the revolver. He didn't aim, he just fired. The first shot hit a car, the second, the building and the third hit Charlie in the chest, knocking him over. Within seconds, Father Bouvier, along with another teacher, came running out of the building, yelling for someone to call 911.

As the priest got close, Pimps waved the pistol at him and told him to stop. Father did, pleading with him, "John, please put down the gun. You're hurt and Charlie's hurt, but nobody else has to get hurt. Please. We'll work this out."

Pimps worked himself into a sitting position, the pistol in his lap. Another jolt of pain hit him and he bent at the waist. Nobody moved and then the sirens sounded. Charlie remained motionless. They stayed that way until the cops showed up. They came out of their car, guns drawn, yelling at Pimps to throw down the weapon and put his hands on top of his head. Pimps obeyed and it was all over in seconds. They rolled Pimps onto his stomach and yanked his hands behind him to cuff him. He screamed with each movement.

"Call an ambulance," the officer attending Charlie said. "This one's got a sucking chest wound and he's losing a lot of blood." Within minutes, the parking lot was filled with cop cars and an ambulance and a fire truck. The school was in lockdown and yellow crime tape went up everywhere. The EMTs covered Charlie's wound with a bandage and loaded him into the ambulance, where they hooked him to an IV bag. A news helicopter hovered overhead.

The cops cuffed Pimps to a gurney and he was loaded into a separate ambulance and taken to the hospital under armed guard. There were by then about fifty officers, city and sheriff's deputies, on site. They started the long process of taking reports from everybody and their brother. Parents had started showing up at the school and were turned away, with the assurance that their children were not hurt.

I had been at a dentist appointment that morning and, by the time I got there, you couldn't get within three blocks of the place. I went home. We turned on the TV and heard there had been a shooting at the school and that two students were injured and being treated at local hospitals, but both were unidentified. Like everyone else in the Quad Cities, we waited. Late in the afternoon, Stone showed up at our door. That's when we found out Charlie had been one of the wounded. Stone knew nothing else, only that he had been taken to the hospital and that the other student was Pimps.

Since Mercy Hospital was the closest to the school, Mom called them first. The hospital acknowledged that a student had been admitted, but since we were not related, they refused to give us any information. Mom then called Charlie's mom to let her know. There was no answer. Dad, Mom and I drove to the hospital and sat around for a couple of hours, mostly being ignored and getting no info. We continued to try to reach his folks without success. We still weren't even sure if Charlie was there.

At about seven in the evening, a nurse came and asked us if we knew how to contact Charlie's parents. Mom gave them Mrs. Settler's phone number. Dad had had enough. He stormed back into the nurses' station and told them Charlie lived with us and that his parents were at least three hours away and we needed to speak to Charlie's doctor.

About thirty minutes later, a man in a business suit came to the waiting room and asked for my father. He led us into an office down the hall and closed the door. "Mr. and Mrs. Williams, we were not able to save Charles. The bullet had nicked his heart and before we could extract the bullet and repair the damage, he died on the operating table. Be assured, we did everything possible." My mom was crying loudly, my crying was not as loud.

The doctor went on, "We have not been able to reach Charles' parents, so the sheriff's department has contacted the sheriff where they live and asked them to notify the family. The body will be released to them after an autopsy is done." He paused for a long minute. "I'm sorry for your loss."

EPILOGUE

We're all scattered to the winds, as the saying goes. Our little group stays in contact but mostly on a once a year basis. Davenport, like probably every city and town in America, has an unofficial homecoming—that time each year where locals are all drawn back. In Davenport's case, it is the Bix Festival. It's a jazz fest kinda thing with this big deal foot race, street fair and old time music. Bix Beiderbecke was this jazz guy who died when he was like 25 and seems to be Davenport's single claim to fame, since they don't want to celebrate the fact that Cary Grant died here.

Anyway, we all gather that weekend when we can. Spouses allowed but not encouraged. I was here with Sandy once, but she had no interest in my high school chums. Rachel came with me the first year we were married and held me when I started crying after our get together, but she has passed on the event ever since. Which is okay, since no mate should ever be subjected to multiple reunions.

We catch up. Share pics of our families. Share news of births and deaths and jobs and life discoveries. We did pretty well for ourselves. Stone, Charles Miller, went to Iowa on his basketball scholarship and had a great freshman year. Was gonna be Iowa's youngest All-American his sophomore year, but he blew out his shoulder and, after a lackluster sophomore year, stopped playing. He came back to the Quad Cities, went to work selling life insurance. He now runs an insurance company and has more money than God. He supports the local church and still goes to all of St. Al's basketball games. I still like him. And secretly love his wife Karen.

Shawn Allen went to Berklee, did okay, and played with an orchestra in St. Louis for a while, then came back to take over his dad's business. He spends most of his time doling out money his family put into a charitable foundation. He plays with a local jazz group and we always get to see him play at the Bix. He got married and has three kids. All of whom play the guitar.

Alan Johnson actually ended up having a great basketball career at Iowa. Got his MBA there and went to work running a suburban newspaper in Columbus, Ohio. He got married as well, has a passel of kids and preaches on Sundays at a big church in Columbus. He's still tall and skinny.

The Denner sisters got married, both to local guys. Both had a kid, both got divorced. Both have jobs and live in the QC. When Erica and I see each other, it is always a hug that lasts too long and a smile that says, "what if." We both know.

We haven't seen Beckett Callaham since we left school, but I heard she ended up going to college at Texas A&M, where she met, fell in love with, and married a Texas cowboy who had a small ranch. And a large inheritance. I hope so. That girl could play some drums. I don't think my brother Tim ever got over her.

Lynne Palmer, Red, died. She was in her twenties, playing professional tennis, and had a seizure in the bathtub and drowned. I heard about it when I was working as a fishing boat mate on the Outer Banks and I celebrated her life by getting pass-out drunk. She was the first girlfriend I ever had and you never really get over your first. Best baseball player I ever knew.

I don't know what happened to Nancy Leggett. She is one of those high school regrets. Sort of a "if I knew then what I know now" kinda memory. I'm sure she has a fine life. I hope so.

I didn't keep up with the squad from DeWitt, though some of them are on Facebook and I'm friends with them there. Most stayed in DeWitt and have led DeWitt lives.

Then there was Olsen and his crew. Pimps was tried as an adult, found guilty of first degree murder and sentenced to life in prison. He testified on his own behalf and that's when we found out Scott Olsen had, in fact, set Charlie up on the car theft thing.

Chubbs had gotten upset when Charlie fired him and Scott convinced him to "pay that jerk back." Charlie's record was posthumously expunged. Last I heard, Pimps was still at Fort Madison State Penitentiary. Chubbs was working at a car wash. Olsen. That fucker was selling used cars. There are few people I wish to die a horrible, painful death. Olsen is one of them.

And Regan. Regan Renarde. Charlie loved her. I would bet my last dollar that when he saw Pimps with that gun, all he was thinking was about protecting Regan. He never told me he loved her, but I knew. And I bet she knew as well. After Charlie died, Regan more or less checked out. She decided not to go to college and instead ended up working on a farm on the island of Kauai in Hawaii. She started singing at the Trees Lounge on the island where she was discovered by a record industry guy. She still lives there but records and has a pretty big following. She doesn't come back to the Quad Cities every year, but when she does, she is feted as our most famous graduate. Rachel was very excited to find out I knew her. Rachel has all her albums. Or whatever they're called now.

Charlie's funeral was a big deal. The school closed and all the students were encouraged to attend. He had saved them all from a mass shooting. I was so pissed, my folks had to banish me to my room for a couple of days. I had lost Charlie. I had let him down. I had not done enough for him. But now, these people who had castigated him, discarded him as a criminal and failure, were singing his praises. I hated it. I hated them. And I hated myself for not saving him. Sure, it was irrational, but I knew, somehow, I could have done more.

Charlie's whole family, except for his stepdad, was there. My folks had them to our house after the funeral. My mom and Mrs. Settler went for a long walk. I never heard about their conversation, but it was a mother thing which I am sure I will never understand. They shared Charlie. And loved him. I hope to God I never have to go through that loss.

J. Woodburn once told me that we are all the heroes of our own stories. I get what he is saying. But I sure wasn't the hero of this part of my story. I will never, ever believe that somehow I didn't let Charlie Settler down. He is the best person I ever knew. I loved him, though I didn't know it, or at least admit it, at the time. I have spent my life trying to be him. Trying to live up to what he would have expected of me. I can't think of him without a stab in my heart, a punch in my gut. I want my son to be him. I want us all to be him.

ACKNOWLEDGEMENTS

The previous *Cutter* book, *Devil's Cut*, was written in response to what a lot of us were feeling about the strange and frightening turn politics had taken in this country. As part of the plot, the country faced a deadly epidemic, but one which was the creation of the mildly warped mind of the author. Little did any of us know we would face such an epidemic two years after the book came out. I assure you, it was not my intention to foretell the future. This book proceeded very slowly in some part because of that epidemic. Sure, there should have been lots of time to write, but my partner felt there were many more pressing projects to address…all involving tools, large and small, which had lain untouched for years. Hopefully, the next issue will arrive sooner.

The team who put this together has done a terrific job. Again. Deborah Varner, the muse, critic, editor, confidante and inspiration, has also acquired the publishing division of AppalachianAcorn and is now also the publisher of the *Cutter* books. Thanks for the vote of confidence. Jordan Callaham took the photo for the cover and Weller Callaham and Aubrey Padgett were the models who graciously agreed to pose. Once again, Tad Barney worked his magic and turned the photo into the cover. If you ever find yourself in need of a caricaturist (and who among us hasn't had that need from time to time), please check out Tad's website for all your caricaturist needs. www.the-nose.com. Patti Hicks once again read the book as it developed and offered valuable insights to the author. He didn't take them all. He probably should have. Finally, to Ken Jones, who in one form or another, has graced several of the *Cutter* books. He is one of those friends the book is dedicated to, but alas, this is the only place he appears in this book. He'll be in the next one. Maybe.

As has become my wont, I borrowed scads of names for my characters. You know, because I'm too lazy to make up more. Those names of real persons borrowed, generally have nothing in common with the characters, so don't confuse them with the real person. In no particular order, Shawn Allen, Dave Bouvier, Charles Robert Miller (Okay, so in this case the real Charlie Miller was the same super athlete as Stone), Tom Reinan, John Peterson, Nancy Leggett, Erica Denner, Erin Denner, Connie (Denner), Alan Johnson, Delia (Segovia), Beckett Callaham, Alex Morgan, Phil Buckle, Coach (Brad) Weaver, Jack Jakubs, Mrs. (Bev) Kenney, and Mrs. (Norma) Dodge. This story of growing up elicited memories which demanded I use names from my younger years. Those include Phil Buckle and Charles Miller, as well as Randy Dunlap (no Andy), Billy Rawers, Tommy Peters and Lynn (no e) Palmer. She did have red hair, she was my first girlfriend in fifth grade, she was one helluva athlete and she did die tragically young. I also used the names of some of my own teachers, Mrs. (Johnnie) Polly, who did kick me out of trig class for tucking in my shirttail; Mr. (Dan) Turner, my fifth grade teacher who was a terrific guy; Mr. Davis, the music man; and my seventh grade English teacher, Mary Margaret Anderson, who taught us everything we ever needed to know about grammar...if we were paying attention. She was truly a nice person. Oh, and finally, in *Devil's Cut*, I forgot to mention another real name I used, Stephen Scott—Sorry, Stephen.

What readers have to say about *Cutter, Cutter Director's Cut* and *Cutter Devil's Cut*:

Cutter

"Mr. Barney's writing is descriptive and witty."

"Excellent book, well written and hard to put down! Very interesting look at behind the scenes politics."

"Cutter is a great debut novel."

"…a fast, magnetic read"

"…a highly satisfying tale"

"A very well written and well thought out story."

"I loved the writing style."

"Barney is a natural storyteller with a talent for character development."

Cutter Director's Cut

"Great sequel. Cutter is a tremendously human character."

"This is a remarkable book by a very talented writer."

"Characters were well defined and captured my interest. A very good read."

"Barney's second novel captures the hilarious and sleazy side of politics and the public sphere."

"Excellent story and character development."

"Cutter is a character with heart."

"Wicked wit."

Kirkus Reviews says of Cutter Director's Cut

"A twisty tale of an ordinary man overcoming treachery."

Cutter Devil's Cut

"Barney has created a delicately balanced plot."

"This Cutter novel is more ambitious in its reach and style than the earlier ones."

"In this *Being There* meets *The Manchurian Candidate* story, Barney delivers more laughs per chapter than some writers inspire in whole books."

"Stumbled across his Cutter books, and glad I did! Straight-shooter writing style."

"Another great effort by this author in the messy life of the lovable character, Cutter!"

"Great book, well written and fun to read. This J. Woodburn Barney is some writer!"

"The balance of comedy and drama makes this a fun read. I'm looking forward to the Netflix original series!"